中国名女人

Famous Chinese Women

The Commercial Press

中国名女人

Famous Chinese Women

First Edition, March 2011

Published by: The Commercial Press (U.S.) Ltd.
The Corporation, 2nd Floor
New York, NY 10013

Famous Chinese Women
Intermediate Readings in Language and Culture

Author : Hong Ziping

Editor: Huang Jiali

ISBN: 978 962 07 1889 2
Printed in Hong Kong

http://www.chinese4fun.net

Contents
目录

PUBLISHER'S NOTE

After studying one to two years of Chinese you have also gained the knowledge of quite a bit of vocabulary. You may be wondering whether there are any other ways for you to further improve your Chinese language proficiency? Although there are a lot of books in the market that are written for people who are studying Chinese it is not easy to find an interesting and easy to read book that matches up to one's level of proficiency. You may find the content and the choice of words for some books to be too difficult to handle. You may also find some books to be too easy and the content is too naive for high school students and adults. Seeing the demand for this kind of learning materials we have designed a series of reading materials, which are composed of vivid and interesting content, presented in a multi-facet format. We think this can help students who are learning Chinese to solve the above problem. Through our reading series you can improve your Chinese and at the same time you will learn a lot of Chinese culture.

Our series includes Chinese culture, social aspects of China, famous Chinese literary excerpts, pictorial symbols of

China, famous Chinese heroes...and many other indispensable aspects of China for those who want to really understand Chinese culture. While enjoying the reading materials one can further one's knowledge of Chinese culture from different angles. The content of the series are contextualized according to the wordbase categorization of HSK. We have selected our diction from the pre-intermediate, intermediate to advanced level of Chinese language learners. Our series is suitable for students at the pre-intermediate, intermediate to advanced level of Chinese and working people who are studying Chinese on their own.

The body of our series is composed of literary articles. The terms used in each article are illustrated with the romanised system called Hànyǔ pīnyīn for the ease in learning the pronunciation. Each article has an English translation with explanation of the vocabulary. Moreover there is related background knowledge in Expansion Reading. Interesting games are added to make it fun to learn. We aim at presenting a three-dimensional study experience of learning Chinese for our readers.

Sì dà měirén

四大美人——

Wáng Zhāojūn

王昭君

Wang Zhaojun — The Four Beauties of China

Wang Zhaojun went to the frontier areas.

Pre-reading Questions

1. In modern China, there are painters who paint for tourists. Have you tried this before?
2. Have you watched any Chinese drama about Wang Zhaojun?

Zhōngguó gǔdài yǒu sìgè zuì yǒumíng de měinǚ Wáng Zhāojūn

❶ 中国古代有四个最有名的美女，王昭君

shì qízhōng zhīyī

是其中之一。

Wáng Zhāojūn xiǎoshíhou jiù zhǎng de hěn měilì hái

王昭君小时候就长得很美丽，还

hěn cōngmíng Shíliù suì de shíhou tā bèi huángdì xuǎn wéi

很聪明。十六岁的时候，她被皇帝选为

qīzi gēn qítā bèi xuǎnzhòng de shàonǚ zhù zài yīqǐ

妻子，跟其他被选中的少女住在一起。

Kěshì huángdì yǒu shùqiān gè qīzi tā bù kěnéng měi

可是，皇帝有数千个妻子，他不可能每

yī gè dōu jiànmiàn yúshì ānpái huàjiā bǎ tāmen de

一个都见面，于是安排画家把她们的

xíngxiàng huà xialai ránhòu gēnjù zhèxiē huà lái tiāoxuǎn
形象画下来，然后根据这些画来挑选
zìjǐ xǐhuan de qīzi Yǒuxiē shàonǚ wèile zǎo yīdiǎn
自己喜欢的妻子。有些少女为了早一点
gēn huángdì jiànmiàn jiù sòng lǐwù gěi huàjiā ràng tā bǎ
跟皇帝见面，就送礼物给画家，让他把
zìjǐ huà de piàoliang yīxiē Wáng Zhāojūn suīrán gè fāngmiàn
自己画得漂亮一些。王昭君虽然各方面
dōu hěn yōuxiù dàn tā bùkěn gěi huàjiā sòng lǐwù
都很优秀，但她不肯给画家送礼物，
jiéguǒ huàjiā bǎ tā huà de hěn píngfán hái gùyì zài tā
结果画家把她画得很平凡，还故意在她
de yǎnjing pángbiān huàle yī gè hēidiǎn shǐ huángdì yīzhí
的眼睛旁边画了一个黑点，使皇帝一直
méiyǒu zhùyì tā
没有注意她。

2 Sān nián hòu Xiōngnú de lǐngxiù láidào shǒudū gēn huángdì
三年后，匈奴的领袖来到首都跟皇帝
jiànmiàn qǐngqiú huángdì wèi tā tiāoxuǎn yī gè měilì de
见面，请求皇帝为他挑选一个美丽的
shàonǚ zuò qīzi Huángdì bùxiǎng gēn Xiōngnú rén dǎzhàng biàn
少女做妻子。皇帝不想跟匈奴人打仗，便
dāying le tā de yāoqiú Huángdì pài rén dào gōngli gēn
答应了他的要求。皇帝派人到宫里，跟
nàxiē děnghòu tā jiējiàn de niánqīng shàonǚ shuō Shuí yuànyì
那些等候他接见的年轻少女说：“谁愿意
jià gěi Xiōngnú lǐngxiù de huángdì biàn rèn tā zuò nǚ'ér
嫁给匈奴领袖的，皇帝便认她做女儿。”

zhèxiē shàonǚ lái dào gōngli jiù xiàng xiǎoniǎo bèi
这些少女来到宫里，就像小鸟被
guān jìn lóngzi yīyàng hènbude mǎshàng fēi chuqu
关进笼子一样，恨不得马上飞出去。

Dàn yī tīngshuō yào dào Xiōngnú de dìfang qù, què méiyǒu
但一听说要到匈奴的地方去，却没有
rén yuànyì. Wèishénme ne? Yīnwèi měi yī gè shàonǚ dōu
人愿意。为什么呢？因为每一个少女都
zhīdào: zhù zài Xiōngnú, yī gè hěn yuǎn de dìfang, qìhòu
知道：住在匈奴，一个很远的地方，气候
hěn lěng, shēnghuó tiáojiàn hěn chà, jià guoqu zhǐ huì yīzhí
很冷，生活条件很差，嫁过去只会一直
chīkǔ.
吃苦。

Zhè shíhou, Wáng Zhāojūn yǒnggǎn de zhàn chulai,
这时候，王昭君勇敢地站出来，
tā jiāndìng de shuō: "Wǒ yuànyì qù." Yúshì, zài
她坚定地说：“我愿意去。”于是，在
huángdì de ānpái xià, Wáng Zhāojūn chéngwéi Xiōngnú lǐngxiù
皇帝的安排下，王昭君成为匈奴领袖
de qīzi, bìngqiě hěnkuài biàn gēnsuí tā líkāi. Zài Wáng
的妻子，并且很快便跟随他离开。在王
Zhāojūn líkāi de yī tiān, huángdì zhōngyú gēn Wáng Zhāojūn
昭君离开的一天，皇帝终于跟王昭君
jiànmiàn le, tā de měilì
见面了，她的美丽
ràng tā hěn chījīng. Huángdì hěn
让他很吃惊。皇帝很
shěbude, dàn yīqiè yǐjing
舍不得，但一切已经
dìng xialai, bùnéng gēnggǎi
定下来，不能更改
le. Huí gōng hòu, tā jiào
了。回宫后，他叫
rén bǎ Wáng Zhāojūn de huà zhǎo
人把王昭君的画找

A playing card with Wang Zhaojun's portrait.

chulai fāxiàn huàjiā jìngrán bǎ tā huàchéng lìng yī gè
出来，发现画家竟然把她画成另一个
yàngzi Huángdì hěn shēngqì jiù bǎ huàjiā shā le
样子。皇帝很生气，就把画家杀了。

Zài Xiōngnú lǐngxiù péibàn xià zhège jiānqiáng de shàonǚ qí
3 在匈奴领袖陪伴下，这个坚强的少女骑
zhe mǎ màozhe lěngfēng yòng le yī nián duō de shíjiān cái
着马，冒着冷风，用了一年多的时间才
láidào Xiōngnú de dìfang Cóngcǐyǐhòu Wáng Zhāojūn gēn
来到匈奴的地方。从此以后，王昭君跟
Xiōngnú rén yīqǐ shēnghuó Suīrán shēnghuó xíguàn hěn bù
匈奴人一起生活。虽然生活习惯很不
yīyàng dàn tā méiyǒu bùmǎn Xiōngnú de xíguàn shì zhàngfu
一样，但她没有不满。匈奴的习惯是丈夫
sǐ hòu qīzi jià gěi bù shì zìjǐ shēng de érzi
死后，妻子嫁给不是自己生的儿子。
Wáng Zhāojūn bù xíguàn dànshì zhàoyàng zuò le Tā hái
王昭君不习惯，但是照样做了。她还
jīngcháng quàngào zìjǐ de zhàngfu yào zhuānxīn guǎnlǐ hǎo
经常劝告自己的丈夫，要专心管理好
zìjǐ de guójiā bùyào gēn Zhōngguó dǎzhàng Zhōngyú Wáng
自己的国家，不要跟中国打仗。终于，王

The tomb of Wang Zhaojun.

Zhāojūn de nǔlì shǐ tā dédào Xiōngnú rén de zūnjìng hé
昭君的努力使她得到匈奴人的尊敬和

zhīchí Zài yǐhòu de liùshí nián li liǎnggè guójiā yīzhí
支持。在以后的六十年里，两个国家一直

bǎochí hépíng méiyǒu fāshēng zhànzhēng
保持和平，没有发生战争。

Translation

❶ There were four great famous beauties in ancient China who are still known to everyone – Wang Zhaojun is one of them.

Wang was already famous for her cleverness and beauty when she was a child. At sixteen, she was taken by the emperor as his wife, and she began to live with the other girls of the same fate in the palace. However, the emperor had thousands of wives and he just could not stay with each and every one of them. Court painters were asked to paint portraits of the girls so that the emperor could choose the women whose pictures appealed most to him. For a better chance to be with the emperor some girls would please the painters with gifts so that they would make them look more beautiful in the picture. Wang was outstanding in every aspect and she was confident of herself, so she did not bribe her painter. As a consequence, the painter painted her portrait with a homely face, and even added a black spot beside her eye on purpose. That picture did not appeal to the emperor.

❷ Three years later, the leader of Xiongnu came to the capital to meet with the emperor. He asked the emperor to give him a beautiful girl as his wife. The emperor did not want to fight the Xiongnu, therefore he agreed to provide him with a wife. The emperor then ordered his men to talk to the wives-to-be and tell them: "Whoever is willing to marry the Xiongnu leader, would be honoured as a princess."

Every girl there could not help feeling like a bird in the cage, and would have liked to fly away whenever there was a chance. But

Xiongnu was not so appealing to them, as they all knew it was a cold, remote place and no joke at all – the bad climate and poor living conditions there would assure a very tough life.

At that moment, the brave Wang stepped forward and declared in a firm voice: "I will go." So under the arrangement of the emperor, Wang became the wife of the Xiongnu leader, and plans were made for her to leave the capital very soon with her new husband. On the day of her departure, the emperor met Wang and was stunned by her beauty. He felt deep regret, but everything was arranged and there was no turning back. When he had returned to the palace, he immediately asked for the portrait of Wang. When he found that she was painted unfaithfully, he was very angry and ordered the painter to be killed.

❸ Accompanied by her Xiongnu husband, the young yet strong-minded woman trekked on horseback to her new home. Their journey took over a year. From then on, she became a part of the Xiongnu people. Although customs were different, she did not complain a bit. It was a Xiongnu custom for a widow to marry her dead husband's son, whom was not born to her. Wang Zhaojun was not used to this custom but she adapted to it. She also asked her husband to put his attention to ruling his country instead of fighting wars with China. In the end, her efforts won the respect and support of the Xiongnu. The two countries lived together in peace, and not a single war broke out in the following sixty years.

Expansion Reading

How Do the Chinese Describe Beautiful Women?

Xi Shi, Diao Chan, Wang Zhaojun and Yang Yuhuan were the Four Renowned Beauties of ancient China. How beautiful were they? – Sunken Fish, Fallen Wild Goose, Hidden Moon, and Shy Flower are four common expressions that people use to describe woman's beauty.

"Sunken Fish" tells the story of Xi Shi who was married to an enemy. Legend has it that when Xi Shi was washing clothes by the stream, the fish was so stunned by the reflection of her beautiful face through the clear water that they forgot to move and sunk to the bottom.

"Fallen Wild Goose" is Wang Zhaojun who was married to a husband in a foreign country. On her farewell journey from her home country to the grassland, she had a lot of emotional reflections, and in order to let her feelings out, she plucked the strings of her pipa and started to play some magnificent but sad songs. When the wild geese in the sky heard the beautiful music and saw the beautiful lady on horseback, they forgot to flutter their wings and fell to the ground.

Xi Shi's portrait on a playing card.

"Hidden Moon" is the description for Diao Chan who saved her country by making use of her beauty as a lure. It was said that she was such a beauty that even the Moon felt humiliated and hid behind the cloud.

"Shy Flower" is for an emperor's beloved woman, Yang Yu Huan. Yang's beauty had made flowers feel shameful and look as if their heads were drooping.

Were these four beauties the most beautiful women in China? Owing to their beauty, they were being used to become spies, get married to solve political problems or become the apples of the rulers' eyes which finally led to political confusion and the country's decline. They were famous women in the politics.

Diao Chan's portrait on a playing card.

GAMES FOR FUN

Rate these Chinese women. How beautiful are they? Rank them from 1 to 3. 1 means the most beautiful and 3 means the least beautiful.

Answers: Open Answers

Dútè de nǚ huángdì

独特的女皇帝——

Wǔ Zétiān

武则天

Wu Zetian — The Unique Empress in Chinese History

Pre-reading Questions

1. Do you agree that women could do any kind of job as well as men?
2. Do you think Wu Zetian is a great empress?

Zài Zhōngguó nǚrén bùnéng zuò huángdì Zhōngguó yóu huángdì

❶ 在中国，女人不能做皇帝。中国由皇帝

guǎnlǐ èrqiān nián zhǐyǒu yī gè nǚ huángdì tā jiàozuò

管理二千年，只有一个女皇帝，她叫做

Officials went on a Journey during Wu Zetian's time.

Wǔ Zétiān Qī shìjì de
武则天。七世纪的

shíhou céngjīng guǎnlǐ Zhōngguó
时候，曾经管理中国

èrshí'èr nián
二十二年。

Wǔ Zétiān xiǎoshíhou de
武则天小时候的

shēnghuó hěn jiānkǔ yǎngchéng tā
生活很艰苦，养成她

Wu Zetian's portrait on a playing card.

yàoqiáng de xìnggé Tā yīnwèi měilì shíduō suì bèi xuǎn
要强的性格。她因为美丽，十多岁被选

jìn huánggōng li dànshì tā de dìwèi hěn dī niánjì
进皇宫里，但是她的地位很低，年纪

yòu xiǎo Bùguò nénggàn de lǎo huángdì xǐhuan tā cōngmíng
又小。不过能干的老皇帝喜欢她聪明，

ràng tā péi zìjǐ dú shū shǐ tā yǒu jīhuì jiēchù dào
让她陪自己读书，使她有机会接触到

zhèngfǔ de wénjiàn zhújiàn liǎojiě zhèngfǔ de gōngzuò Tā hái
政府的文件，逐渐了解政府的工作。她还

dú le xǔduō píngshí méiyǒu jīhuì dú de shū zēngzhǎng
读了许多平时没有机会读的书，增长

le zhīshi Hòulái lǎo huángdì bìng le tā de érzi lái
了知识。后来老皇帝病了，他的儿子来

kàn fùqīn de bìng jīngcháng jiàndào Wǔ Zétiān liǎng gè
看父亲的病，经常见到武则天，两个

niánqīngrén chǎnshēng le gǎnqíng bìng tōutōu de wǎnglái Lǎo
年轻人产生了感情，并偷偷地往来。老

huángdì sǐ hòu tā de érzi zuò le xīn de huángdì
皇帝死后，他的儿子做了新的皇帝。

Kěshì ànzhào dāngshí huánggōng de guīdìng Wǔ Zétiān shì lǎo
可是按照当时皇宫的规定，武则天是老

huángdì de qīzi zhīyī yòu méiyǒu háizi bùnéng liúzài
皇帝的妻子之一，又没有孩子，不能留在
huánggōng yào dào miàoli shēnghuó
皇宫，要到庙里生活。

❷ Lǎo huángdì sǐ de shíhou Wǔ Zétiān cái èrshí duō
老皇帝死的时候，武则天才二十多
suì Tā bùxiǎng yīshēngrén dōu zài miàoli guò jìmò de
岁。她不想一生人都在庙里，过寂寞的
shēnghuó suǒyǐ hěn bù kuàilè Yīnián hòu xīn huángdì
生活，所以很不快乐。一年后，新皇帝
dào miàoli shāoxiāng Wǔ Zétiān bǎwò zhècì jīhuì
到庙里烧香。武则天把握这次机会，
qiānfāngbǎijì jiàndào huángdì kūzhe shuō hěn xiǎngniàn tā
千方百计见到皇帝，哭着说很想念他，
ràng xīn huángdì fēicháng gǎndòng Yīnwèi tā běnlái shì lǎo
让新皇帝非常感动。因为她本来是老
huángdì de qīzi xīn huángdì xiǎng le hěnduō bànfǎ cái
皇帝的妻子，新皇帝想了很多办法，才
ràng Wǔ Zétiān huídào huánggōng
让武则天回到皇宫
li Bùjiǔ Wǔ Zétiān
里。不久，武则天
wèi xīnhuángdì shēng le gè
为新皇帝生了个
nǚ'ér Huánghòu qù kàn tā
女儿。皇后去看她，
tā zài huánghòu líkāi zhīhòu
她在皇后离开之后，
shāsǐ zìjǐ de nǚ'ér
杀死自己的女儿，
què shuō shì huánghòu shā de
却说是皇后杀的。

Wu Zetian subsidized the construction of Longmen Fengxian Temple.

Huángdì hěn shēngqì jiù gǎnzǒu huánghòu ràng Wǔ Zétiān
皇帝很生气，就赶走皇后，让武则天
zuò le xīn huánghòu Huángdì bù xǐhuan gōngzuò shēntǐ yòu
做了新皇后。皇帝不喜欢工作，身体又
chà Wǔ Zétiān jiù dài tā bànshì Wǔ Zétiān shì gè yǒu
差，武则天就代他办事。武则天是个有
cáinéng de rén yòu gēn lǎo huángdì xuéguo hěnduō dōngxi
才能的人，又跟老皇帝学过很多东西，
suǒyǐ guójiā guǎnlǐ de hěn hǎo yòngle hěnduō yǒu nénglì
所以国家管理得很好，用了很多有能力
de dàchén
的大臣。

Wǔ Zétiān bìng bù zhǐ xiǎng zuò huánghòu tā dàochù sànbù
❸ 武则天并不只想做皇后，她到处散布
nǚrén kěyǐ zuò huángdì de yìlùn Yīnwèi hěnduō rén fǎnduì
女人可以做皇帝的议论。因为很多人反对
tā tā yòng hěnduō cánkù de dàchén bǎ fǎnduì tā de
她，她用很多残酷的大臣，把反对她的
rén dōu zhuāle shā le bāokuò tā de jǐgè érzi
人都抓了杀了，包括她的几个儿子。
Zhōngyú méiyǒu rén zài gǎn fǎnduì tā Zài liùshíqī suì nà
终于没有人再敢反对她。在六十七岁那
yī nián Wǔ Zétiān rènwéi shíjī chéngshú le zhèngshì dāng
一年，武则天认为时机成熟了，正式当
shàngle huángdì Qíguài de shì shíwǔ nián hòu Wǔ Zétiān
上了皇帝。奇怪的是，十五年后，武则天
kuàiyào sǐ què xuānbù bù zuò huángdì sǐle zhīhòu réngrán
快要死，却宣布不做皇帝，死了之后仍然
yǐ huánghòu de shēnfen zàng zài zhàngfu de mù páng Tā
以皇后的身份，葬在丈夫的墓旁。她
méiyǒu àn jìhuà ràng xìng Wǔ de qīnrén dāng huángdì réngrán
没有按计划让姓武的亲人当皇帝，仍然

yóu tā de érzi zuò huángdì
由她的儿子做皇帝。

Suǒyǒu huángdì sǐ hòu dōu huì zài mù qián lì yī kuài
所有皇帝死后，都会在墓前立一块

bēi bēi shàng xiě yīshēng de chéngjiù Zhǐyǒu Wǔ Zétiān méiyǒu
碑，碑上写一生的成就。只有武则天没有

zhèyàng zuò tā yào dà chén wèi tā lìle yī kuài bēi
这样做，她要大臣为她立了一块碑，

dànshì shàngmian méiyǒu wénzì Zhè yī kuài wúzìbēi gěi rén
但是上面没有文字。这一块无字碑，给人

xǔduō xiǎngxiàng de kōngjiān Yǒurén shuō tā bǎ zìjǐ de
许多想象的空间。有人说，她把自己的

gōngláo huò guòcuò jiāogěi lìshǐ
功劳或过错，交给历史

lái pínglùn Jīntiān zhèkuài bēi
来评论。今天这块碑

hái zài Xī'ān Duì zhège dútè
还在西安。对这个独特

de nǚrén nǐ huì zěnyàng pínglùn
的女人，你会怎样评论

ne
呢？

The blank tablet in front of Wu Zetian's grave.

Translation

❶ In China the throne was not for women. During its two thousand years of history, China was only once ruled by a woman – Wu Zetian. This happened in the 7th century. Empress Wu ruled China for twenty-two years.

Wu Zetian had a bad childhood so she grew up to be a tough person. Because of her extraordinary beauty she was sent to the palace when she was thirteen. She was young and her rank was very low. However, the old emperor liked this smart young girl so much that he asked her to wait on him when he studied. Because of this, Wu had the chance to read government documents and learned how the government worked. She also read many books that she would otherwise not have had access to, so her knowledge grew immensely during this period. Later on, the emperor got sick and his son came to see him often. The two young people met and soon fell in love, but they kept their affair a secret. When the emperor died, his son became the new emperor. But according to the rules of the palace, as she was one of the wives of the old emperor and bore him no children, Wu was required to leave the palace and live in a temple.

❷ Wu was only twenty something when the old emperor died. She was very sad. She did not want to spend the rest of her life in a temple. She could not bear the loneliness. A year later, the new emperor made a pilgrimage to the temple. Wu seized the chance and found a way to meet him. She cried bitterly and told the emperor that she missed him very much. The emperor was deeply moved. It was not easy at all to get her back to the palace, as she had been the consort of the old emperor, but somehow he managed to arrange it. Not long after, Wu bore the emperor a baby girl, and the queen came to see her and her new-born baby. After she had left Wu killed her own daughter but lied to the emperor that it was the queen who'd done it. The emperor was so angry that he sent the queen away and let Wu take her place. Since the emperor was not interested in his work and his health was poor, Wu worked for him. She was talented in politics because she had learned a lot about the government while she was attending the old emperor. As a consequence, she ran the country very well, and made many able people ministers.

❸ Being the queen alone did not satisfy Wu Zetian; she wanted to be the emperor. She thought women could do the job as well as men, so she initiated talk about it all over the country. When people spoke out against her ideas, she asked many cruel ministers to arrest them. The people that she killed included her own sons. Since the killings, no one dared to say no to her again. When she turned sixty-seven, Wu thought it was time she claimed the throne and so she acted. But fifteen years later when she was dying, she surprised everyone by announcing she would step down from the throne and expressed her wish to be buried beside her husband as the queen when she died. In the end, she passed the throne to her son rather than to a member of her maternal family as planned.

It was a practice that a stone tablet with an inscription of the emperor's lifelong achievements be erected in front of his grave. However, Empress Wu made an exception – she had a tablet erected in front of her grave, but ordered that no inscription be made. The blank tablet stimulates the imagination. Some people think that she did not want to comment on herself but to leave that to the historians. The tablet is still there in Xi'an. Pay a visit to it when you are there. But about this extraordinary woman, what do you think?

Expansion Reading

Queen Mother Lü and Queen Mother Xiao

Queen Mother is an emperor's mother or grandmother. In Chinese history there were many queen Dowagers who participated in politics under the banner of assisting the new and young emperor. Besides Wu Zetian, there were also the famous Queen Mother Lü and Queen Mother Xiao.

Queen Mother Lü was the first woman politician who seized power by assisting the emperor. She was the wife of Emperor Liu Bang of the Han dynasty. Liu was only a district official when Lü married him. In the days when Liu was on the war field struggling for power, Lü suffered a lot for her husband – being imprisoned as her husband's substitute, and being held as captive by his husband's enemy. Then Liu became the emperor, but the political situation was not stable in the early days of his reign. To help his husband to secure his power, Lü swept away the dissidents in the court. After the Emperor had died, Queen Mother Lü took the reins of government by claiming to assist the weak little emperor. During her reign, Lü not only killed many ministers who had helped her husband gain the throne, but also killed the royal clans except her own. She wished that her maternal family could rule the country forever, but her plan never worked out.

Not only did queen Mothers in the Han clan participated in politics, those in ethnic minorities also followed suit. A thousand years later, there was another queen Mother called Xiao. Compared to Lü, Xiao was intelligent and just. She came from an important family. Because her father had once helped the emperor, the emperor married her as a way of giving back. When Xiao was thirty, the emperor died. The new emperor was so young that Xiao had to assist him in ruling. She headed the government for forty years. Xiao was humble and sincere, and she knew well how to manage people. Under her ruling, the economy and culture of the country developed to new heights. She was also an expert in warfare. She had issued commands in the field and won some wars. One may say that she was a woman general.

GAMES FOR FUN

Use a few Chinese words to write down what you think about Wu Zetian on the blank stone tablet.

Answers: Suggested Answers: 美丽, 要强, 残酷, 聪明

Zuì yǒumíng de nǚ shīrén

最有名的女诗人——

Lǐ Qīngzhào

李清照

Li Qingzhao — The Most Famous Woman Poet in China

Pre-reading Questions

1. Why did few women receive good education in ancient China?
2. Are you fond of Chinese ancient poetry?

Zài gǔdài Zhōngguó hěn shǎo nǚzǐ yǒu jīhuì dúshū Zài

1 在古代中国，很少女子有机会读书。在

wénxué shang yǒu chéngjiù de jiù gèngjiā shǎo le Lǐ Qīngzhào

文学上有成就的，就更加少了。李清照

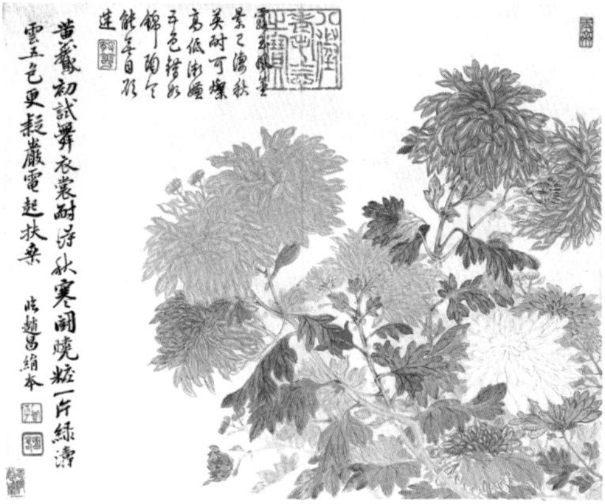

Yellow chrysanthemums conveyed the poetic image of human weakness in one of Li Qingzhao's famous poems.

shì zuì yǒumíng de nǚ shīrén dú tā de shī dōu huì bèi
是最有名的女诗人，读她的诗都会被
tā de àiqíng gùshi gǎndòng
她的爱情故事感动。

Lǐ Qīngzhào de fùqīn shì guānyuán yě shì hěn yǒumíng
李清照的父亲是官员，也是很有名
de zuòjiā ér mǔqīn yě hěn xǐhuan xiěshī Shòu tāmen
的作家，而母亲也很喜欢写诗。受他们
de yǐngxiǎng Lǐ Qīngzhào hěnxiǎo jiù dǒngde xiěshī Tā de
的影响，李清照很小就懂得写诗。她的
shī xiě de hěn hǎo dédào hěnduō rén de chēngzàn
诗写得很好，得到很多人的称赞。

Shíbā suì de shíhou Lǐ Qīngzhào jiéhūn Tā de
十八岁的时候，李清照结婚。她的
zhàngfu míngjiào Zhào Míngchéng bǐ tā niánzhǎng sān suì shì
丈夫名叫赵明诚，比她年长三岁，是
yī gè gāojí guānyuán de érzi Tāmen de xìnggé hěn
一个高级官员的儿子。他们的性格很
xiāngsì dōu xǐhuan xiěshī jīngcháng yīqǐ tǎolùn xiěshī
相似，都喜欢写诗，经常一起讨论写诗
de jìqiǎo Cǐwài Zhào Míngchéng àihào shōují zhēnguì
的技巧。此外，赵明诚爱好收集珍贵
de shūhuà hé kèzài shí hé jīnshǔ shàng de gǔ wénzì
的书画和刻在石和金属上的古文字，
Lǐ Qīngzhào bùdàn zhīchí tā hái gēn tā yīqǐ zhěnglǐ
李清照不但支持他，还跟他一起整理
hé yánjiū Yǒu yī nián Zhào Míngchéng bù zàijiā Lǐ
和研究。有一年，赵明诚不在家，李
Qīngzhào hěn xiǎngniàn tā xiěle yī shǒu shī jì gěi tā
清照很想念他，写了一首诗寄给他。
Zhào Míngchéng kàndào tā de shī hòu fēicháng gǎndòng Tā
赵明诚看到她的诗后，非常感动。他

hěn xīnshǎng zhè shǒu shī yě xīwàng zìjǐ néng xiěchu yī
很欣赏这首诗，也希望自己能写出一
shǒu gèng hǎo de Tā huā le sān tiān shíjiān xiěle wǔshí
首更好的。他花了三天时间，写了五十
duō shǒu shī zài bǎ tāmen gēn Lǐ Qīngzhào de shī fàngzài
多首诗，再把它们跟李清照的诗放在
yīqǐ wèn péngyou nǎ yī shǒu zuìhǎo Péngyou kàn wán
一起，问朋友哪一首最好。朋友看完
hòu xiǎngle yīhuì biàn shuō Zěnme kàn háishi zhè
后，想了一会，便说：“怎么看，还是这
shǒu shī xiě de zuì měi ya Yuánlái tā tiāoxuǎn de nà shǒu
首诗写得最美呀！”原来他挑选的那首
shī jiùshì Lǐ Qīngzhào xiě de Zhào Míngchéng suīrán hěn
诗，就是李清照写的。赵明诚虽然很
shīwàng què wèi Lǐ Qīngzhào de cáinéng gǎndào gāoxìng
失望，却为李清照的才能感到高兴。

Shíduō nián hòu Zhào Míngchéng de fùqīn yīnwèi zhèngzhì
2 十多年后，赵明诚的父亲因为政治
dòuzhēng shībài bèi shā Wèile zhuānxīn xiězuò yī běn yánjiū
斗争失败被杀。为了专心写作一本研究
gǔdài wénzì de shū Zhào Míngchéng juédìng huídào jiāxiāng
古代文字的书，赵明诚决定回到家乡
jūzhù Wèile zhīchí zhàngfu Lǐ Qīngzhào bùdàn xiézhù
居住。为了支持丈夫，李清照不但协助
tā xiě shū hái yuànyì guòzhe jiǎndān de shēnghuó bǎ
他写书，还愿意过着简单的生活，把
dà bùfen de qián huā zài yánjiūshang Zhèyàng píngjìng de
大部分的钱花在研究上。这样平静的
shēnghuó guòle hěnduō nián zhídào fāshēngle zhànzhēng tāmen
生活过了很多年，直到发生了战争，他们
cái líkāi jiāxiāng táo dào nánfāng qù Kěxī láidào
才离开家乡，逃到南方去。可惜，来到

nánfāng bùjiǔ Zhào Míngchéng tūrán shēngbìng sǐ le Gèng
南方不久，赵明诚突然生病死了。更
bùxìng de shì liǎng rén duō nián shōují de zhēnguì shūhuà
不幸的是，两人多年收集的珍贵书画，
dàbùfen gěi qiángdào qiǎng qù
大部分给强盗抢去。

Wèile shēnghuó Lǐ Qīngzhào bèipò jià gěi yī gè
为了生活，李清照被迫嫁给一个
guānyuán Zhège guānyuán qǔ tā zhǐshì wèile dédào nàxiē
官员。这个官员娶她，只是为了得到那些
zhēnguì de shūhuà Tā nénggòu chéngwéi guānyuán yě shì yòng
珍贵的书画。他能够成为官员，也是用
bù héfǎ de shǒuduàn délái Nà shíhou zhàngfu wéifǎn
不合法的手段得来。那时候，丈夫违反
fǎlǜ qīzi shuōle chulai yě yào
法律，妻子说了出来也要
yīqǐ zuòláo de Lǐ Qīngzhào shì yī
一起坐牢的。李清照是一
gè hěn zhèngyì de rén tā zhīdàole
个很正义的人，她知道了
xīn zhàngfu de mìmì hòu bù tīng
新丈夫的秘密后，不听
péngyou de quàngào jiānchí yào bǎ tā
朋友的劝告，坚持要把他
de shìqing gōngkāi Jiéguǒ liǎng gè
的事情公开。结果，两个
rén dōu zuòláo le Yī duàn cuòwù
人都坐牢了。一段错误
de hūnyīn bùzú sān gè yuè biàn
的婚姻，不足三个月便
jiéshù
结束。

This inscription was included in *Jin Shi Lu* compiled by Li Qingzhao's husband.

Dédào qīnrén de bāngzhù Lǐ Qīngzhào zuòle jiǔtiān de láo
❸ 得到亲人的帮助，李清照坐了九天的牢

biàn chūlai le Tā shīqùle suǒyǒu zhēnguì de shūhuà
便出来了。她失去了所有珍贵的书画，

shēnghuó biàn de hěn kùnnan Yóuyú tā jià guò liǎng cì
生活变得很困难。由于她嫁过两次，

hěnduō péngyou dōu kànbuqǐ tā bùkěn tígōng bāngzhù Lǐ
很多朋友都看不起她，不肯提供帮助。李

Qīngzhào hěn nánguò dàn tā méiyǒu hòuhuǐ zìjǐ zuòguo de
清照很难过，但她没有后悔自己做过的

shì Tā bǎ shēnghuó shang de yīqiè tòngkǔ hé gǎnshòu dōu
事。她把生活上的一切痛苦和感受，都

xiě jìn tā de shīli
写进她的诗里。

Hòulái de rìzi Lǐ Qīngzhào yīzhí yī gè rén
后来的日子，李清照一直一个人

shēnghuó Tā hěn xiǎngniàn Zhào Míngchéng wèi tā xiěxiale
生活。她很想念赵明诚，为他写下了

hěnduō zhùmíng de shī Chúle xiěshī Lǐ Qīngzhào hái yòng
很多著名的诗。除了写诗，李清照还用

jǐnián de shíjiān bǎ Zhào Míngchéng wèi wánchéng de shū xiě
几年的时间，把赵明诚未完成的书写

chulai Zhèběn shū bāohánle Zhào Míngchéng yǔ Lǐ Qīngzhào de
出来。这本书包含了赵明诚与李清照的

mèngxiǎng
梦想。

Translation

❶ Few women had a chance to receive an education in ancient China, not to mention opportunities to excel in literature, yet there were a few success stories. Among them Li Qingzhao is a household name. She is the most important woman poet of all time. The love stories that she tells in her poems are so touching that they can easily move readers to tears.

Li was born into a poetry-loving family. Her father was a famous writer and worked as an official while her mother wrote poems for pleasure. Under their influence, Li showed her talent for poetry as a child. She wrote well, and her works achieved wide acclaim.

When she reached eighteen, Li got married. Her husband, Zhao Mingcheng, was the son of a high-ranking official and three years older. The couple had much in common; they were both poets, and they often shared their views on poetry. Zhao was also very interested in collecting famous paintings, works of calligraphy, ancient stone and metal tablets with inscriptions. Li loved her husband and admired his work, and so she helped him with research and editing. Zhao once had to leave home for a year and Li missed him so much that she sent him a poem, a beautifully written love poem. Zhao was deeply moved after reading it. He liked the poem very much but hoped that he could make one even better. Having spent three days finishing fifty or so poems, Zhao mixed Li's up with his own, and asked his friend which poems was the best. "In all aspects, this one is definitely the best!" remarked his friend, after reading all the works. Needless to say, the poem that his friend picked out was the one by Li. Though he was very disappointed, Zhao felt proud of his talented wife.

❷ A decade or so later, Zhao's father was killed in a political conflict. Zhao decided to move back to his ancestral home to focus on writing a book on the study of ancient inscriptions. In support of her husband, Li offered her help in writing, and they began to lead a simple life in order to save most of their money for their work. They lived peacefully for many years until war broke out. The couple left their home and fled to the South where it was safer. Unfortunately, not long after they arrived at their destination, Zhao suddenly caught a disease and passed away. To make things even worse, bandits robbed them of most of the valuable works of art that they had been collecting over the years.

Hoping that it would make life easier, Li married an official whom she did not love. This man did not love her either, and only married her for her valuable art collection. He was not a decent man; he got his job illegally. At that time, if a man committed a crime, the wife had to go to prison with her husband too, no matter if it was she who turned him in. Li was a person of integrity, and she chose to disclose her new husband's secret, though her friends urged her not to do so. As a consequence, the newlyweds were sent to prison, and thus ended the short-lived marriage by mistake within three months.

❸ However, with the help of her family, the poet was set free nine days later. Life became even harder since she had lost all of her valuables. And as she had been married twice, many of her friends looked down upon her. They did not even give her a hand when she was in need. Though she was saddened by it, she did not regret what she had done. From then on her poems reflected her innermost feelings of suffering.

For the rest of her life Li lived alone. She missed Zhao so much that she wrote many poems in memory of him. These poems have all become classics. Besides poetry, Li also spent several years finishing her husband's book, and thus realized their mutual dreams. Their book is still highly regarded by people today.

Expansion Reading

Cai Wenji – A Female poet in Xiongnu

Men were more important than women in ancient China. Therefore, only the daughters from well-to-do families had the chance to receive education. Even in such unfavorable conditions, there were some women who had great talent in literature. Besides Li Qingzhao, Cai Wenji was another prominent figure.

Cai Wenji was a poet living in 2 A.D., a time full of political turmoils.

Her father was a famous scholar and calligrapher, so she loved studying and poetry since childhood. In addition, her skills on the zither were remarkable. When she was sixteen, she got married, but her husband died of illness within a year. To make things even worse, her father also died in prison soon. Now Cai had nothing left to lose but her own self in the unstable society. During an attack by foreign soldiers, she was kidnapped to Xiongnu, and was forced to marry a leader there. She was only twenty-three and from then on she had been living in pain. But somehow she had learned to play the "hujia", a musical instrument similar to a flute. However, she still missed her home country very much. With the memories of her life in China she wrote the classic "Eighteen Movements of the Hujia".

The return of Wenji to Han.

Fortunately, when a good friend of his father's learned that she was stranded in Xiongnu, he redeemed her from her husband. Cai was already thirty-five when she came back to China. She got married again. Her husband had committed a serious crime in the second year of their marriage. In a messy manner, she went to Cao Cao to beg him off. Cao Cao said it was no use begging him because the order had been issued. But Cai Wenji was eloquent and she succeeded in persuading Cao Cao to send speed horse messenger and cancel the order. At last, her husband was set free. She recited 400 essays she had read and won the respect of all the guests.

GAMES FOR FUN

Here is the first line of Li Qingzhao's poem:

寻寻觅觅　冷冷清清　凄凄惨惨戚戚.

Count the number of repetition words. Apart from these words, how many repetition words can you give?

Answers: 7, Open Answers

Fǎngzhī dà wáng Huáng Dàopó

纺织大王——黄道婆

Huang Daopo — The Master Weaver

Pre-reading Questions

1. Have you ever tried to fight for your dream?
2. Have you ever seen the high-quality fabric products in South China?

Zhībù shì Zhōngguó gǔdài fùnǚ de rìcháng gōngzuò yě shì
❶ 织布是中国古代妇女的日常工作，也是
hěnduō jiātíng de shōurù láiyuán Shuōqǐ zhībù Zhōngguórén
很多家庭的收入来源。说起织布，中国人
yīdìng xiǎngqǐ yī gè lǎonǎinai tā jiàozuò Huáng Dàopó
一定想起一个老奶奶，她叫做黄道婆。

Huáng Dàopó shì qībǎi niánqián de rén tā de jiā
黄道婆是七百年前的人，她的家
zài jīntiān Shànghǎi de fùjìn Yīnwèi shēnghuó kùnnan
在今天上海的附近。因为生活困难，
tā shí'èr suì jiù bèi mài gěi biéren dāng qīzi Láidào
她十二岁就被卖给别人当妻子。来到
zhàngfu jiā zhīhòu báitiān tā yào dào nóngtián li gōngzuò
丈夫家之后，白天她要到农田里工作，

wǎnshang háiyào zhībù
晚上 还要 织布

dào shēnyè Xīnkǔ
到 深夜。辛苦

yīdiǎn dào méi shénme
一点 倒 没 什么，

dànshì zhàngfu hé jiāli de
但是 丈夫 和 家里 的

Songjiang, Huang Daopo's home town, is famous for its high quality cotton cloth.

rén bǎ tā dàngzuò gōngrén bù shì dǎ jiùshì mà Yǒu yī
人 把 她 当做 工人，不 是 打 就是 骂。有 一

cì Huáng Dàopó yòu bèi tāmen dǎ le yīdùn hái guān
次，黄 道婆 又 被 他们 打 了 一顿，还 关

zài fángjiānli bùxǔ chī dōngxi Tā zàiyě bùnéng rěnshòu
在 房间里 不许 吃 东西。她 再也 不能 忍受

le juéxīn táo chūqu xúnzhǎo xīn de shēnghuó Bànyè tā
了，决心 逃 出去 寻找 新 的 生活。半夜，她

zài wūdǐng lòngle yī gè dòng pá chūlai duǒzài yītiáo tíng
在 屋顶 弄了 一 个 洞 爬 出来，躲在 一条 停

zài jiāngbiān de chuánshang
在 江边 的 船上 。

2 Dì-èr tiān zǎochen jiāngbiān de yī tiáo chuán zhèng zhǔnbèi
第二 天 早晨，江边 的 一 条 船 正 准备

hángxíng Hūrán chuánshang chūxiànle yī gè sǎnzhe tóufa
航行。忽然，船上 出现了 一 个 散着 头发、

liǎnsè cāngbái de niánqīng nǚzǐ Tā guì zài chuán de zhǔrén
脸色 苍白 的 年轻 女子。她 跪 在 船 的 主人

miànqián qǐngqiú tā bǎ tā zài dào nánfāng zhège nǚzǐ
面前，请求 他 把 她 载 到 南方，这个 女子

jiùshì Huáng Dàopó Wèishénme tā xiǎng qù nánfāng ne
就是 黄 道婆。为什么 她 想 去 南方 呢？

Yuánlái zhèxiē nián lái tā xǐhuan shàng zhībù de gōngzuò
原来 这些 年 来，她 喜欢 上 织布 的 工作，

měitiān dōu yánjiū zěnyàng cáinéng zhī chū měilì de bù lái
每天都研究怎样才能织出美丽的布来。
Yǒu yī cì tā zài shìchǎng shang kàndào cóng nánfāng yùn lái
有一次，她在市场上看到从南方运来
de bù yánsè hé pǐnzhì dōu hěn hǎo ràng tā shífēn
的布，颜色和品质都很好，让她十分
xǐ'ài Cóngcǐ tā yǒule yī gè mèngxiǎng dào nánfāng
喜爱。从此，她有了一个梦想：到南方
qù xuéxí fǎngzhī jìshù Yóuyú zhàngfu hé jiāli de rén
去学习纺织技术！由于丈夫和家里的人
bǎ tā bī de wúlùkězǒu tā juédìng mǎshàng jiù táo dào
把她逼得无路可走，她决定马上就逃到
nánfāng qù shíxiàn tā de mèngxiǎng Chuán de zhǔrén tīng
南方去，实现她的梦想。船的主人听
wán tā de huà hòu fēicháng tóngqíng tā biàn dāying tā de
完她的话后，非常同情她，便答应她的
qǐngqiú
请求。

Jiù zhèyàng Huáng Dàopó láidào nánfāng Dāngdìrén
就这样，黄道婆来到南方。当地人

Modern weaving tool.

zhīdào tā yī gè rén láidào zhèlǐ dōu hěn rèqíng de
知道她一个人来到这里，都很热情地
jiēdài tā Tāmen gěi tā gèzhǒng bāngzhù bìng bǎ tāmen
接待她。他们给她各种帮助，并把他们
de fǎngzhī jìshù yīdiǎn dōu méiyǒu bǎoliú de jiāo tā Huáng
的纺织技术一点都没有保留地教她。黄
Dàopó cōngmíng hàoxué hěnkuài jiù xuéhuì zhèxiē jìshù
道婆聪明好学，很快就学会这些技术，
zhújiàn chéngwéi yī gè yōuxiù de zhībù zhuānjiā Tā zài
逐渐成为一个优秀的织布专家。她在
nánfāng shēnghuóle jiējìn sānshí nián yīzhí guò de hěn hǎo
南方生活了接近三十年，一直过得很好。
Dànshì shíjiān yītiānyītiān guòqù tā yùláiyù xiǎngniàn
但是，时间一天一天过去，她愈来愈想念
zìjǐ de jiāxiāng
自己的家乡。

❸ Zhōngyú Huáng Dàopó dàole lǎonián de shíhou gàobié le
终于，黄道婆到了老年的时候，告别了
nánfāng huídào jiāxiāng Zhè shíhou jiāxiāng de fǎngzhī
南方，回到家乡。这时候，家乡的纺织
jìshù réngrán hěn luòhòu rénmen de shēnghuó hěn pínkǔ
技术仍然很落后，人们的生活很贫苦。
Wèile shǐ jiāxiāng de rénmen shēnghuó de gèng hǎo Huáng
为了使家乡的人们生活得更好，黄
Dàopó gùbushàng zìjǐ niánjì dà le shēntǐ bùhǎo
道婆顾不上自己年纪大了，身体不好，
nàixīn de bǎ zìjǐ de jìshù jiāogěi tāmen Zhè qījiān
耐心地把自己的技术教给他们。这期间，
tā yībiān jiāo tāmen yòng xīnshì de gōngjù zhībù yībiān
她一边教他们用新式的工具织布，一边
gǎigé zhěnggè gōngxù Tā hái chuàngzào yītào xīnxíng de
改革整个工序。她还创造一套新型的

zhībù gōngjù shǐ shēngchǎn xiàolǜ tígāo jǐ bèi cāozuò
织布 工具，使 生产 效率 提高 几 倍，操作
qǐlái yě fēicháng fāngbiàn Yīduàn shíjiān zhīhòu Sōngjiāng
起来 也 非常 方便。一段 时间 之后，松江
yīdài de rénmen dōu xuéhuì Huáng Dàopó de xīn jìshù
一带 的 人们 都 学会 黄 道婆 的 新 技术，
yě xǐhuan shǐyòng tā fāmíng de xīn gōngjù Tāmen de
也 喜欢 使用 她 发明 的 新 工具。他们 的
shēngchǎnliàng bùdàn tígāo le zhī chulai de bù yě bǐ
生产量 不但 提高 了，织 出来 的 布 也 比
guòqù piàoliang duō le Sōngjiāng de zhībù zài quánguó gègè
过去 漂亮 多 了。松江 的 织布 在 全国 各个
dìfang dōu dà shòu huānyíng rénmen de shēnghuó cóngcǐ dédào
地方 都 大 受 欢迎，人们 的 生活 从此 得到
hěn dà de gǎishàn
很 大 的 改善。

Huáng Dàopó huídào gùxiāng de jǐnián zhōng yīzhí
黄 道婆 回到 故乡 的 几年 中，一直
mángzhe zhībù de shì cónglái méiyǒu xiǎngshòu guò Tā
忙着 织布 的 事，从来 没有 享受 过。她

Ancient women weaved their cloth.

sǐ hòu rénmen dōu hěn shāngxīn dàjiā còu chūqián lái wèi
死后，人们都很伤心，大家凑出钱来为

tā jiànzào yī zuò miào jìniàn tā wèi jiāxiāng zuòguo de
她建造一座庙，纪念她为家乡做过的

shì Yǒurén hái bǎ tā jiāo rén zhībù de gùshi biānchéng
事。有人还把她教人织布的故事编成

gēqǔ ràng értóng měitiān chàngzhe
歌曲，让儿童每天唱着。

Translation

❶ Weaving was part of a woman's daily chores in ancient China; it was also the main source of income for families. When it comes to weaving, the Chinese people always remember an old nanny called Huang Daopo.

Huang Daopo lived about seven centuries ago by the river Songjiang. Her family was very poor and she was sold to a family as a child bride when she was only twelve. However, her life as a wife was even harder. In the day time she worked on the farm and from evening until late at night she had to weave. She could stand the hard work, but she could not tolerate the torture meted out by her husband and her in-laws. They saw her only as a slave laborer. They cursed her and beat her whenever they felt like it. Once Huang was beaten up and locked in a room without food. She decided she had had enough and it was time she took a chance for freedom. In the middle of the night, she made a hole in the ceiling and climbed out. She fled to the riverside and hid in a boat that anchored there.

❷ The next morning when the boat was ready to set sail, the boatmen saw before them a young woman with a pale face and loose hair. She knelt before the master and begged him to take her to the South. Needless to say, she was Huang Daopo. She wanted to go to the South because during all those years as a weaver she had become more and more interested in her work. Every day she looked at the fabric that she wove, and wondered how she could weave even more beautiful ones. She had once found different kinds of fabric from the South in the market. These had very good quality and beautiful colors, and they appealed to her greatly. From that moment on, she had a dream: Go to the South to learn weaving. Now that she had no future with her husband and her in-laws, she made up her mind to escape to the South where she could realize her dream. The master was moved by her story and agreed to take her with them to the South.

Thus Huang went to the South. When the people there learned that she had come alone, they gave her a warm welcome. They not only helped her in many ways, but also taught her all the weaving techniques that they knew. Huang was a fast and hard-working learner, and in no time she mastered all the techniques and became an expert. She lived in the South for nearly thirty years. Life was very good there, but as time went by she missed more and more of her home – Songjiang.

❸ When Huang became an old woman, it was time for her to bid farewell to the Southern country and return to Songjiang. At that time the weaving techniques in her hometown were still very backward. To improve their livelihood Huang taught them all she knew with great patience, disregarding her old age and weak body. She taught them techniques for using new weaving tools, and she also revised all the steps in weaving fabrics. She further invented a new set of weaving tools which were much easier to use. Production became more efficient. After some time, the people of the Songjiang region mastered the new techniques taught by Huang, and they also employed the tools that she invented. As a consequence, not only was production increased, but the quality of their fabric also improved. The fabrics from Songjiang became very famous all over the country, and the people's quality of life advanced.

Since coming back to Songjiang, Huang was always busy in her work. She never took a rest. All of her time and energy were put in her work. When she died, people there were very sad. To commemorate her they gathered money to build a temple in her name. There were even songs written about her. Children would sing them every day. These songs have also come down to the present day.

Expansion Reading

Legend has it that the ultimate ancestor of the Chinese people — Huang Di was a great inventor and her wife, Lei Zu, was the first woman who taught the Chinese people to domesticate silkworms and collect the silk threads.

Huang Di and Lei Zu were born five thousand years ago. At that time, people might go naked. It did not look good and they could not keep warm by covering their bodies with only leaves and feathers. Legend has it that Lei Zu saw that some silkworms on mulberry trees were spinning cocoons. She took some home, soaked them in water, and unwound the threads. Then she hung the silk fibers to dry, detangled them, and carefully spun them into a piece of silk fabric. When it was finished she wrapped it around her body happily and went out to show it to others. Everybody thought it was very beautiful and praised Lei Zu for her talent. Through long-time observation and many experiments Lei Zu had learned about the life cycle of silkworms and had mastered the know-how of spinning, of which she shared with the people there.

Her story spread fast and wide. Lei Zu was praised as the "Goddess of Sericulture" for her contribution.

Nobody knows if this legend is true. But it is true that Chinese people knew how to domesticate silkworms and collect the silk threads in early times. And it had been a custom for the Emperor's wife to perform the annual ceremony of domesticating silkworms.

GAMES FOR FUN

Look at the pictures and choose from below: remove cotton seeds, buy the cotton, spin the cotton, wash the cotton seeds.

(a)

(b)

Answers: (a) spin the cotton (b) buy the cotton

Hǎo tàihòu Xiàozhuāng
好太后——孝庄

Xiaozhuang — The Good Queen Mother

Pre-reading Questions

1. How many emperors did Xiao Zhuang helped?
2. Have you ever watched any TV programs or movies about Xiao Zhuang?

---

1 Tàihòu shì huángdì de mǔqīn
太后是皇帝的母亲
huòzhě zǔmǔ.
或者祖母。
Zhōngguó zuìhòu yī gè
中国最后一个
cháodài kāishǐ de shíhou yǒu yī
朝代开始的时候有一
gè hǎo tàihòu, jiéshù de shíhou
个好太后，结束的时候
yǒu yī gè huài tàihòu. Xiànzài
有一个坏太后。现在
wǒmen yào jiǎng de shì hǎo tàihòu
我们要讲的是好太后

Xiao Zhuang's portrait.

de gùshi Tā jiàozuò Xiàozhuāng tā bāngzhùle liǎng gè
的 故事。她 叫做 孝庄，她 帮助了 两 个
huángdì shǐ Zhōngguó chéngwéi yī gè qiángdà de guójiā
皇帝，使 中国 成为 一 个 强大 的 国家。

Sānbǎiduō nián qián Xiàozhuāng zài cǎoyuán chūshēng shíjǐ
三百多 年 前，孝庄 在 草原 出生，十几
suì jiù hé jiějie yīqǐ jià dào pángbiān de guójiā liǎng
岁 就 和 姐姐 一起，嫁 到 旁边 的 国家，两
gè rén dōu jià gěi guówáng de érzi zuò qīzi Tā niánjì
个 人 都 嫁 给 国王 的 儿子 做 妻子。她 年纪
tài xiǎo le zhàngfu yòu yǒu wǔ gè qīzi suǒyǐ bù tài
太 小 了，丈夫 又 有 五 个 妻子，所以 不 太
zhùyì tā
注意 她。

Dāngshí de Zhōngguó hěn ruò lǎo guówáng xiǎng
当时 的 中国 很 弱，老 国王 想
dàitì Zhōngguó de huángdì tǒngzhì zhèpiàn tǔdì jiù fādòng
代替 中国 的 皇帝 统治 这片 土地，就 发动
zhànzhēng Kěshì zhànzhēng méiyǒu jiéshù lǎo guówáng biàn
战争。可是 战争 没有 结束，老 国王 便
sǐ le Xiàozhuāng de zhàngfu chéngle xīn de guówáng Xīn
死 了，孝庄 的 丈夫 成了 新 的 国王。新
guówáng jìxù gēn Zhōngguó dǎzhàng érqiě shènglì le zuòle
国王 继续 跟 中国 打仗，而且 胜利 了，做了
Zhōngguó de huángdì
中国 的 皇帝。

Xīn guójiā chénglì bùjiǔ huángdì biàn tūrán bìngsǐ le
❷ 新 国家 成立 不久，皇帝 便 突然 病死 了。
Yóuyú láibují ānpái jìchéngrén zhèngfǔ yīpiàn hùnluàn
由于 来不及 安排 继承人，政府 一片 混乱，
hěnduō rén zhēngzhe zuò huángdì Qízhōng jīhuì zuìgāo de
很多 人 争着 做 皇帝。其中 机会 最高 的，

shì huángdì de yī gè dìdi Tā zài zhànchǎng shang lìguo
是皇帝的一个弟弟。他在战场上立过

hěnduō gōngláo zhǎngwò le guójiā de jūnshì lìliang Kěshì
很多功劳，掌握了国家的军事力量。可是

gēnjù Zhōngguó de xíguàn huángdì sǐ le shì érzi jìchéng
根据中国的习惯，皇帝死了，是儿子继承

de Zhè shíhou Xiàozhuāng yīfāngmiàn zhēngqǔ dàchén de
的。这时候，孝庄一方面争取大臣的

zhīchí yīfāngmiàn shuōfú tā bùyào zuò huángdì Zhōngyú
支持，一方面说服他不要做皇帝。终于，

zài Xiàozhuāng de ānpái xià tā de liù suì de érzi dāng
在孝庄的安排下，她的六岁的儿子当

shàng huángdì liǎng gè rén yīqǐ xiézhù xiǎo huángdì
上皇帝，两个人一起协助小皇帝。

Qíshí shūshu yīzhí xiǎng dàitì xiǎo huángdì zhǐshì
其实，叔叔一直想代替小皇帝，只是

bèi Xiàozhuāng yòng gèzhǒng fāngfǎ zǔzhǐ Jǐnián hòu shūshu
被孝庄用各种方法阻止。几年后，叔叔

bìngsǐ le Xiàozhuāng cái fàng le xīn Tā yīzhí zài bèihòu
病死了，孝庄才放了心。她一直在背后

zhīchí huángdì tíchū hěnduō jiànyì shǐ guójiā jiànjiàn
支持皇帝，提出很多建议，使国家渐渐

wěndìng xiàlai
稳定下来。

Shíjǐ nián hòu tā niánqīng de érzi què tūrán sǐqù bā
❸ 十几年后，她年轻的儿子却突然死去，八

suì de sūnzi dāng shàng huángdì Yúshì zhège sūnzi jiù gēn
岁的孙子当上皇帝。于是这个孙子就跟

tàihòu yīqǐ shēnghuó jiēshòu tā yángé de jiàoyù Zài tā
太后一起生活，接受她严格的教育。在她

de yǐngxiǎng xià xiǎo huángdì hěn xǐhuan dúshū Wúlùn rènhé
的影响下，小皇帝很喜欢读书。无论任何

shíhou zhǐyào ná qǐ shū
时候，只要拿起书，

tā jiù huì bǎ yīqiè shìqing
他就会把一切事情

dōu wàngjì Yī gè nǚrén
都忘记。一个女人，

Yī gè xiǎohái chángcháng bèi
一个小孩，常常被

dàchén qīfu yào guǎnlǐ hǎo
大臣欺负，要管理好

yī gè dà guójiā hěn bù
一个大国家，很不

róngyì Tàihòu jīngcháng jiāo
容易。太后经常教

Xiao Zhuang put great effort in educating her grandson, Kang Xi.

tā guǎnlǐ guójiā de fāngfǎ hé chǔlǐ shìqing de dàoli
他管理国家的方法和处理事情的道理。

Tàihòu bāngzhù xiǎo huángdì shā le zuì yǒu quánlì de dàchén
太后帮助小皇帝杀了最有权力的大臣，

xiǎo huángdì zhōngyú zài shísì suì de shíhou qīnzì guǎnlǐ
小皇帝终于在十四岁的时候，亲自管理

guójiā Bùguò yùshàng zhòngdà shìqing tā dōu huì zhǔdòng
国家。不过，遇上重大事情，他都会主动

wèn tàihòu de yìjiàn Zài tāmen de nǔlì xià guójiā
问太后的意见。在他们的努力下，国家

yuèláiyuè qiángdà
越来越强大。

Tàihòu sǐ de shíhou yǐjing qīshíyī suì le
太后死的时候，已经七十一岁了。

Huángdì wèile péizhe kuàiyào sǐqù de tàihòu tā jǐtiān
皇帝为了陪着快要死去的太后，他几天

dōu bù chīfàn shuìjiào Tàihòu sǐ hòu huángdì méiyǒu ràng
都不吃饭睡觉。太后死后，皇帝没有让

tā shīwàng Tā chéngwéi Zhōngguó lìshǐ shang zhùmíng de hǎo
她 失望。他 成为 中国 历史 上 著名 的 好

huángdì Kāngxī huángdì Kěyǐ shuō tā nénggòu zuòchu
皇帝——康熙 皇帝。可以 说，他 能够 做出

zhèxiē chéngjiù gēn tàihòu de jiàoyù shì fēn bù kāi de
这些 成就，跟 太后 的 教育 是 分 不 开 的。

Translation

❶ Queen Dowager is the king's mother or grandmother.

At the beginning of the last dynasty in China, there was a good Queen Dowager while a bad Queen Dowager emerged at the end. Now, the story begins with a good Queen Dowager whose name was Xiaozhuang. She helped two kings to rule China, making China very strong.

About three hundred years ago, Xiaozhuang was born in a grassland. In her teens, she and her sister both married a son of that country's king. She was too young to get the attention of her husband who already had five wives.

At that time China was very weak. The old king waged war against China, aiming to become king of China instead. However, he died before his war succeeded, and Xiaozhuang's husband became the new king. The new king went on with the war. He won and became the king of China.

❷ Not long after the new dynasty was established, the king suddenly died. Since he had not appointed a successor beforehand, the court was in chaos, and many people struggled for power. One of the king's younger brothers had a very good chance to become the successor. He had won many wars and was in charge of the armies. But according to the Chinese custom, it was the son who succeeded the throne. At this moment, she tried to gain the support of the ministers and at the same time talked the younger brother out of taking the throne. In the end, Xiaozhuang's son became the king in her arrangement. Xiaozhuang and the younger brother worked together to help the little king rule the country.

This was not what the little king's uncle wished, and he always plotted to replace the young king. But he failed every time as Xiaozhuang would do anything to stop him. Some years later the uncle died and Xiaozhuang was relieved. She helped the little king behind the scene. She made a lot of suggestions and helped the country to stabilize.

❸ After a decade or so her young son suddenly passed away. Xiaozhuang's eight-year-old grandson succeeded the throne. This young child had been living with his grandmother and had received a very good education with strict discipline. Under her influence, the young king loved studying. He was so obsessed with books that whenever he was reading he would forget everything. A woman and a child were often bullied by the ministers. Ruling a big country well is no easy job. The Queen Dowager often taught the young king methods and theories of ruling a country. The Queen Dowager helped the young king to kill the most powerful minister. So, at the age of fourteen, the young king was allowed to reign over the country alone. Yet he would still ask for the Queen Dowager's opinions about big issues. With their mutual efforts, the country became stronger and stronger.

The Queen Dowager passed away at the old age of seventy-one. When she was dying, the king was so worried about her that he stayed beside her deathbed without eating and sleeping for days. After her death, the young king did not let her down. He was regarded as one of the best emperors in Chinese history – Emperor Kangxi. One may say that he owed his success to the good upbringing by his grandmother.

Expansion Reading

Xiaozhuang and Emperor Kangxi

Emperor Kangxi was the grandson of Empress Xiaozhuang. Under his ruling, China reached new heights in many aspects in history.

Kangxi had been living with his grandmother since childhood. Her good upbringing to the young emperor is the main reason why Xiaozhuang is such a respectable figure in history. The upbringing that she gave Kangxi had fostered his ability to manage the country and deal with people. Xiaozhuang was also very concerned with every detail. Kangxi's good habits and conduct owed a lot to her serious training.

Influenced by his nanny, Kangxi once got into the habit of smoking when he was a boy. Xiaozhuang was very worried about it. She warned and advised him against it until he gave it up. After he had succeeded the throne, Kangxi forbade anyone in the government from smoking. If he knew anyone who smoked he would ask them to stop it.

Xiaozhuang was also the role model for the young emperor. Kangxi did not like drinking alcoholic as he knew well it would damage a person's health. He thought that a drunken man could not remain sober, and over drinking would even make a person stupid. Therefore after he had become the emperor he would consciously remind himself not to drink. Even when celebrating the festivals he would only have a drop of it. He had kept this good habit for his whole life.

Xiaozhuang was also very concerned about Kangxi's behavior. She demanded that he mind his decorum on all occasions. Emperor Kangxi later told his children and grand-children: "From the first day on the throne, I have always dressed properly, sat properly, no matter I am discussing state affairs with my ministers or talking with you about family matters. This has been a habit since my childhood." Under his serious education, Kangxi's offspring were mostly brilliant.

Huài tàihòu Cíxǐ

坏太后——慈禧

Cixi — The Bad Queen Mother

Cixi's portrait.

Pre-reading Questions

1. Cixi is a controversial historical figure. Do you agree that she is a bad Queen Dowager?
2. Yihe Yuan is a beautiful royal garden. Have you ever visited this palace?

Cíxǐ shì Zhōngguó zuìhòu yī gè tàihòu Tā suīrán méiyǒu

❶ 慈禧是中国最后一个太后。她虽然没有

zuò huángdì dàn tǒngzhì le Zhōngguó wǔshí nián

做皇帝，但统治了中国五十年。

Cíxǐ zài shíliù suì de shíhou chéngwéi huángdì

慈禧在十六岁的时候成为皇帝

de qīzi Yīnwèi gěi huángdì shēng le yī gè érzi

的妻子。因为给皇帝生了一个儿子，

yīncǐ huángdì hěn xǐhuan tā Nà shíhou huángdì jīngcháng

因此皇帝很喜欢她。那时候，皇帝经常

shēngbìng zhèngfǔ de gōngzuò yòu duō shǐ tā yìngfù bù

生病，政府的工作又多，使他应付不

lái Tā zhīdào Cíxǐ de zì xiě de hěn hǎo jiù bǎ

来。他知道慈禧的字写得很好，就把

zìjǐ gěi dàchén men de zhǐshì gàosu tā yóu tā xiě
自己给大臣们的指示告诉她，由她写
xialai Jiù zhèyàng Cíxǐ jiànjiàn shúxī le zhèngfǔ de
下来。就这样，慈禧渐渐熟悉了政府的
shìwù hái dǒngde le guǎnlǐ guójiā de jìqiǎo
事务，还懂得了管理国家的技巧。

Huángdì bìngsǐ hòu Cíxǐ liù suì de érzi dāng
皇帝病死后，慈禧六岁的儿子当
le xīn huángdì Huángdì sǐ qián ānpái le bā gè dàchén
了新皇帝。皇帝死前安排了八个大臣
lái xiézhù xīn huángdì dàn tāmen dōu xiānhòu bèi Cíxǐ
来协助新皇帝，但他们都先后被慈禧
shāsǐ Cíxǐ zài bèihòu kòngzhì zhe xiǎo huángdì zhújiàn bǎ
杀死。慈禧在背后控制着小皇帝，逐渐把
quánlì jízhōng zài zìjǐ shǒushang Hòulái zhège huángdì
权力集中在自己手上。后来，这个皇帝
bù dào èrshí suì jiù bìngsǐ le Cíxǐ yòu zhǎo le yī
不到二十岁就病死了，慈禧又找了一
gè sì suì de háizi dāng huángdì Dāngrán bùguǎn shuí zuò
个四岁的孩子当皇帝。当然，不管谁做
huángdì zhēnzhèng de quánlì dōu zài Cíxǐ de shǒushang
皇帝，真正的权力都在慈禧的手上。

❷ Cíxǐ dédào quánlì hòu hěn zhòngshì xiǎngshòu Jùshuō tā
慈禧得到权力后，很重视享受。据说她
měitiān de shēnghuófèi yào jǐwàn liǎng Zhè fèiyong yǒu duō
每天的生活费，要几万两。这费用有多
gāo Gàosu nǐ ba dāngshí Zhōngguó xiàng wàiguó gòumǎi yī
高？告诉你吧，当时中国向外国购买一
sōu xiānjìn de zhànjiàn yào èrshíwǔ wàn liǎng
艘先进的战舰，要二十五万两。

Zài Cíxǐ liùshí suì nànián Rìběn gēn Zhōngguó
在慈禧六十岁那年，日本跟中国

dǎzhàng Nà shíhou Cíxǐ zhèng máng zhe jiànzào yī gè
打仗。那时候，慈禧 正 忙 着 建造 一 个

yuánlín lái qìngzhù shēngri Zhège yuánlín míngjiào Yíhéyuán
园林 来 庆祝 生日。这个 园林 名叫 颐和园，

zào de hěn piàoliang huā de qián yě hěnduō yào sānqiānwàn
造 得 很 漂亮，花 的 钱 也 很多，要 三千万

liǎng Hòulái qián bùgòu le Cíxǐ jiù bǎ gòumǎi zhànjiàn
两。后来 钱 不够 了，慈禧 就 把 购买 战舰

de qián ná lái yòng Zhànzhēng yùláiyù jīliè hěnduō
的 钱 拿 来 用。 战争 愈来愈 激烈，很多

dàchén qǐngqiú tā tíngzhǐ gōngchéng bǎ qián yòng lái dǎzhàng
大臣 请求 她 停止 工程，把 钱 用 来 打仗。

Cíxǐ hěn shēngqì hái shuō Jīntiān ràng wǒ bùmǎn de
慈禧 很 生气，还 说：“今天 让 我 不满 的

rén wǒ huì ràng tā huó bù xiàqù
人，我 会 让 他 活 不 下去！”

Qiánfāng de zhànzhēng yīzhí zài jìnxíng zhe Cíxǐ
前方 的 战争 一直 在 进行 着，慈禧

yīdiǎn dōu bù guānxīn Tā zài gōng li jiēshòu dàchén men de
一点 都 不 关心。她 在 宫 里 接受 大臣 们 的

zhùhè hái liánxù kàn le sān tiān xì Zhōngyú zhànzhēng
祝贺，还 连续 看 了 三 天 戏。终于，战争

shībài le Wèile jìxù xiǎngshòu
失败 了。为了 继续 享受，

Cíxǐ jìngrán tóngyì qiāndìng yī
慈禧 竟然 同意 签订 一

Yi Heyuan in Beijing.

tiáo fēicháng bù píngděng de tiáoyuē shǐ Zhōngguó péile hěnduō
条非常不平等的条约，使中国赔了很多
qián shīqùle yī dà piān tǔdì
钱，失去了一大片土地。

Xiāoxi chuánchū hòu rénmen dōu hěn fènnù Niánqīng
❸ 消息传出后，人们都很愤怒。年轻
de huángdì juédìng lìyòng gǎigé lái qǔhuí quánlì Kěxī
的皇帝决定利用改革来取回权力。可惜
jìhuà shībài Cíxǐ bǎ huángdì guān qilai hái tíngzhǐ
计划失败，慈禧把皇帝关起来，还停止
jìnxíngle sāngè yuè de gǎigé Nà shíhou wàiguórén dōu
进行了三个月的改革。那时候，外国人都
zhīchí gǎigé Cíxǐ yīzhí dōu bù xǐhuan tāmen biàn ràng
支持改革，慈禧一直都不喜欢他们，便让
míxìn de lǎobǎixìng bǎ wàiguórén gǎnzǒu Jiéguǒ hěnduō
迷信的老百姓把外国人赶走。结果，很多
wàiguórén bèi shā bā gè guójiā zǔchéng liánhé jūnduì gēn
外国人被杀，八个国家组成联合军队跟
Zhōngguó dǎzhàng Zhànzhēng hěnkuài jiéshù Zhōngguó yòu bèi
中国打仗。战争很快结束，中国又被
dǎbài Wàiguó jūnduì jìnrù Běijīng de shíhou Cíxǐ
打败。外国军队进入北京的时候，慈禧

Yuanmingyuan in Beijing.

dàizhe huángdì táo dào xī'ān qù Wèile huídào gōngli tā
带着皇帝逃到西安去。为了回到宫里，她

zài yī cì qiāndìng wánquán bù píngděng de tiáoyuē péile gèng
再一次签订完全不平等的条约，赔了更

duō de qián hái shīqùle hěnduō guójiā de quánlì
多的钱，还失去了很多国家的权利。

Cíxǐ huídào Běijīng hòu méi guò jǐnián biàn sǐ
慈禧回到北京后，没过几年便死

le Zài tā de tǒngzhì xià Zhōngguó biàn de hěn qióng
了。在她的统治下，中国变得很穷，

lǎobǎixìng de shēnghuó yùláiyù kǔ Wèile gǎibiàn zhège
老百姓的生活愈来愈苦。为了改变这个

guójiā hěnduō rén jiārù gémìng Zài Cíxǐ sǐ hòu dì-sān
国家，很多人加入革命。在慈禧死后第三

nián gémìng chénggōng le Zhōngguó cóngcǐ méiyǒule huángdì
年，革命成功了，中国从此没有了皇帝。

Translation

❶ Queen Dowager Cixi was the last Queen Dowager in Chinese history. Although she did not claim the throne, she ruled China for fifty years.

Cixi became a wife of the emperor when she was sixteen. The emperor liked her very much because she was beautiful and bore him a son. However, the emperor got sick often and could not handle the many responsibilities of government work. He knew that Cixi's handwriting was good, so he asked her to write down his instructions to the ministers. Gradually Cixi became familiar with government affairs, and she even learned the ways of managing a country.

After the emperor died, Cixi's six-year-old son became the new emperor. Before his death, the old emperor had arranged eight high-ranking ministers to assist the new emperor. However, they were killed by Cixi one by one. Cixi was ambitious in politics, she controlled the child emperor behind his back, and step by step she amassed power. The emperor died of a serious illness before he was twenty. After his death, Cixi found a four-year-old to take his place. Of course, no matter who sat on the throne, the one who had the real power was Cixi.

❷ Cixi saw her personal enjoyment as the most important thing once power was in her hands. It is said that her daily expenses amounted to many thousands of teals. To get an idea of how much this amount meant, at that time, a new and well-equipped warship that China brought from a foreign country cost 250,000 teals.

When Cixi was sixty, Japan waged war against China. At the time Cixi was busy building a garden to celebrate her birthday. The garden named Yihe Xuan, was very beautiful, and yet it cost a tremendous amount of money – thirty million teals in total. When the garden project was running short of money, Cixi ordered that the funds reserved for warships be used. As the war became more intense, many ministers urged her to stop the project and put the money back in the war effort. Cixi became angry, saying: "Whoever makes me unhappy today, I will not let him take one more breath!"

❸ When the news was out, people were very angry. The young emperor decided to get his power back by way of political reforms. Unfortunately his plan failed and he was locked up by Cixi. The reform that had been going on for three months came to a full stop. However, foreigners in China all supported the reform movement. Cixi hated them, and she encouraged the superstitious Chinese to kick them out of China. As a result, many foreigners were killed, and eight strong nations formed an alliance to fight a war against China. The war did not last long, and China was beaten again. When the alliance troops entered Peking, Cixi fled to the North with the emperor. In order to get back to her comfortable palace, she signed a ridiculously unequal treaty again. That meant China would be losing more money and surrendering more rights to others.

Several years after she had returned to Peking, Cixi died. Under her reign, China became a very poor country, and people's lives became tougher. Many more people joined the revolution in order to change their country. Three years after her death, the revolution succeeded, and there were no more emperors in China.

Expansion Reading

Ruler behind blinds

"Ruling behind blinds" was a way used by empresses when they wanted to assist the young emperors in managing national affairs. When the queen Dowager had to meet with the ministers, vertical blinds would be set before her seat. This system was used in many dynasties.

There were many "Rulers behind blinds" in history. Before she took the throne, Empress Wu had once ruled behind blinds. But the woman who ruled the longest time in this way was the famous Queen Dowager Cixi. She made use of this system to manipulate two emperors for half a century.

But why did the ruling empress have to hide behind blinds? It was done to show that the Emperor was the real ruler. Moreover, they had to keep a proper distance from men. This was especially true for the women of high society. When a woman had to meet with a man other than her family members, she would ask her maid to pass on her message rather than talk with him face to face. She might also talk to him with windows or screens set between them. As for the prestigious queen Dowager, the ritual was even more rigid to make sure that her face would not be seen by the men at the other side. However, sometimes the empress had to receive the documents submitted by the ministers, listen to their suggestions, or give them orders. In these cases hanging blinds were much more convenient than windows, curtains, or screens. The empress no longer needed to pass on her messages through her maids of honor but could deal with the ministers more efficiently. The blinds had dual meanings: firstly, they made sure that there was no direct contact between the empress and her male underlings, and secondly, the empress could show to her subjects that she had no intention to reign over the country directly.

Gémìng nǚ yīngxióng

革命女英雄——

Qiū Jǐn

秋瑾

Qiu Jin — The Heroine of the Revolution

Qiu Jin's statue.

Pre-reading Questions

1. Imagine you were a Chinese in the late 1800's. How would you have felt when you had witnessed the revolution?
2. Can you name two women who are famous for their leading roles in the women's movement in China?

---

❶ Zài Zhōngguó zhǐyào dú guò jìndài lìshǐ dōu rènshi
在中国，只要读过近代历史，都认识
Qiū Jǐn Tā shì gémìngjiā yě shì tuīdòng fùnǚ yùndòng
秋瑾。她是革命家，也是推动妇女运动
de nǚ yīngxióng
的女英雄。

Qiu Jin's home town, Shao Xing.

Yībāqīwǔ nián Qiū Jǐn chūshēng zài yī gè bǐjiào
一八七五年，秋瑾出生在一个比较
fùyù de jiātíng li Tā hěnxiǎo jiù xǐhuan wénxué
富裕的家庭里。她很小就喜欢文学，
zuì àikàn gǔdài nǚ yīngxióng de gùshi Qiū Jǐn de
最爱看古代女英雄的故事。秋瑾的
gèxìng rèqíng jiù xiàng nánháizi yīyàng Tā jīngcháng chuān
个性热情，就像男孩子一样。她经常穿
nánrén de yīfu zuò nánrén xǐhuan de yùndòng hái xuéxí
男人的衣服，做男人喜欢的运动，还学习
gōngfu Dāngshí de Zhōngguó hěn ruò zhèngfǔ de guǎnlǐ hěn
功夫。当时的中国很弱，政府的管理很
chà lǎobǎixìng de shēnghuó hěn kǔ Qiū Jǐn hěn dānxīn
差，老百姓的生活很苦。秋瑾很担心
guójiā de qiántú tā xīwàng zìjǐ xiàng gǔdài de nǚ
国家的前途，她希望自己像古代的女
yīngxióng yīyàng nénggòu bāngzhù zìjǐ de guójiā
英雄一样，能够帮助自己的国家。

Èrshí suì nà nián Qiū Jǐn jiēshòu le fùqīn de
二十岁那年，秋瑾接受了父亲的
ānpái gēn yī gè shāngrén jiéhūn Dànshì tā hěnkuài jiù
安排，跟一个商人结婚。但是，她很快就
fāxiàn zhàngfu shì yī gè píngfán zìsī kànqīng nǚrén de
发现丈夫是一个平凡、自私、看轻女人的
nánrén Tā zhǐ kǎolǜ zìjǐ de lìyì duì guójiā de
男人。他只考虑自己的利益，对国家的
shìqing yīdiǎn dōu bù guānxīn Jiéhūn bùjiǔ tāmen biàn
事情一点都不关心。结婚不久，她们便
jīngcháng chǎojià Gēn zhèyàng de nánrén yīqǐ shēnghuó Qiū
经常吵架。跟这样的男人一起生活，秋
Jǐn gǎndào hěn tòngkǔ
瑾感到很痛苦。

❷ Jǐ nián hòu Qiū Jǐn yǔ zhàngfu láidào Běijīng shēnghuó
几年后，秋瑾与丈夫来到北京生活。
Nà shíhou Zhōngguó gēn bā gè guójiā dǎzhàng shū le
那时候，中国跟八个国家打仗输了，
wàiguó jūnduì gānggāng líkāi Běijīng dàochù yīpiàn hùnluàn
外国军队刚刚离开北京，到处一片混乱。
Qiū Jǐn měitiān dōu máng zhe bāngzhù nàxiē shīqù qīnrén de
秋瑾每天都忙着帮助那些失去亲人的
lǎobǎixìng gēn zhàngfu de máodùn yùláiyù dà
老百姓，跟丈夫的矛盾愈来愈大。

Zhōngyú zài jiéhūn hòu de dì-bā nián Qiū Jǐn juédìng
终于，在结婚后的第八年，秋瑾决定
líkāi jiātíng dào Rìběn de Dōngjīng liúxué Dāngshí de
离开家庭，到日本的东京留学。当时的
Dōngjīng shì Zhōngguó gémìng de huódòng jīdì Qiū Jǐn yī
东京，是中国革命的活动基地。秋瑾一
dào nàli biàn jiēshòu le gémìng de sīxiǎng tā jījí
到那里，便接受了革命的思想。她积极
cānjiā liúxuéshēng de huódòng dàochù xuānchuán gémìng hái
参加留学生的活动，到处宣传革命，还
chénglì le zìjǐ de gémìng zǔzhī
成立了自己的革命组织。

Qiū Jǐn zài Rìběn liúxué bùjiǔ Zhōngguó zhèngfǔ biàn
秋瑾在日本留学不久，中国政府便
yāoqiú xuésheng huíguó Huíguó hòu Qiū Jǐn zài yī jiā
要求学生回国。回国后，秋瑾在一家
nǚzǐ xuéxiào dāng lǎoshī Tā bāngzhù le hěnduō yǒu kùnnan
女子学校当老师。她帮助了很多有困难
de fùnǚ hái bàn le yī fèn bàozhǐ gàosu tāmen yào
的妇女，还办了一份报纸，告诉她们要
zhēngqǔ gēn nánrén píngděng de quánlì Zhè duàn shíjiān
争取跟男人平等的权利。这段时间，

Qiū Jǐn yīzhí mìmì de zhǔnbèi gémìng Tā liánluò quánguó
秋瑾一直秘密地准备革命。她联络全国

gèdì de gémìng huǒbàn hái zǔzhī jūnduì jìnxíng xùnliàn
各地的革命伙伴，还组织军队，进行训练。

Jīngguò yī duàn shíjiān de zhǔnbèi Qiū Jǐn rènwéi jīhuì dào
❸ 经过一段时间的准备，秋瑾认为机会到

le biàn fādòng gémìng Kěxī zhèngfǔ zhīdào le tāmen
了，便发动革命。可惜，政府知道了她们

de jìhuà hái bǎ lìng yī chù de gémìng lǐngxiù zhuāzhù
的计划，还把另一处的革命领袖抓住

le Suīrán qíngkuàng hěn wēixiǎn Qiū Jǐn háiyǒu chōngzú
了。虽然情况很危险，秋瑾还有充足

de shíjiān líkāi Dànshì Qiū Jǐn gēn huǒbàn men shuō
的时间离开。但是，秋瑾跟伙伴们说：

Gémìng yào yǒu liúxuè cái huì chénggōng de Tā bù
“革命要有流血，才会成功的。”她不

jiēshòu quàngào ràng suǒyǒu rén líkāi hòu zìjǐ yī gè
接受劝告，让所有人离开后，自己一个

rén liúzài jīdì li Zhèngfǔ de jūnduì hěnkuài jiù gǎn
人留在基地里。政府的军队很快就赶

guòlái zhuāzǒu le tā
过来，抓走了她。

Qiū Jǐn bèi
秋瑾被

zhuō hòu yīzhí bùkěn
捉后，一直不肯

gēn zhèngfǔ hézuò Jǐtiān
跟政府合作。几天

hòu Qiū Jǐn zài lǎobǎixìng
后，秋瑾在老百姓

de miànqián bèi shāsǐ
的面前被杀死

Qiu Jin's tomb.

le Nànián tā cái sānshí'èr suì Sǐ qián tā biǎoxiàn
了。那年，她才三十二岁。死前，她表现
de hěn jiānqiáng hái zuò le yī shǒu shī biǎoshì zìjǐ
得很坚强，还作了一首诗，表示自己
juébù hòuhuǐ Qiū Jǐn de sǐ ràng lǎobǎixìng rènshi le
绝不后悔。秋瑾的死，让老百姓认识了
gémìng gèng duō rén jiārù le gémìng de duìwu Sìnián
革命，更多人加入了革命的队伍。四年
hòu gémìng chénggōng le Qiū Jǐn de lǐxiǎng zhōngyú shíxiàn
后，革命成功了，秋瑾的理想终于实现。

Translation

❶ Qiu Jin was a very famous figure who helped shape modern China. She was not only a revolutionary who tried to overturn the Qing Empire, she was also a pioneer who led the women's movement in China.

Qiu Jin was born into a well-to-do family in 1875. As a child she loved literature, especially the stories of heroines of the ancient world. She was an enthusiastic girl but behaved like a boy. She liked to dress in men's clothes, played men's sports, and even learned kung fu. China was then a very weak country; the governance was bad, and the life of the people was poor. Qiu was very worried about the future of her country. She wished she could help China like the heroines in the past.

When Qiu was twenty she accepted her father's arrangement and married a businessman. But very soon she found out that her husband was only a mediocre, selfish man who looked down upon women. His main concerns were his own personal benefits; the affairs of state were none of his concern. They began to fight not long after they were married. Qiu felt living with such a man was like torture.

❷ After several years, Qiu Jin moved to Peking with her husband.

At that time every corner of Peking was in chaos – China was in disarray because of the war against the Eight-Nation Alliance. When they arrived in the capital, the foreign troops had just left. Every day Qiu was busy helping people who had lost their families during the war while her relationship with her husband grew ever worse.

After eight years of marriage, Qiu decided to leave her family and go to Tokyo to study. Tokyo was then the base of China's revolutionaries. Qiu readily accepted the revolution's thoughts the moment she set foot in Japan. She proactively took part in the Chinese student activities, joined the propaganda tours, and founded her own revolution organization.

However, not long after she arrived in Japan, the Qing government ordered all the students to return home. Back in China, Qiu found a teaching post at a girls' school. There, she offered her help to many women who had difficulties. She also published a newspaper, telling women that they had to fight for equal rights for themselves. During that period, Qiu was secretly helping to organize the revolution. She contacted fellow-revolutionaries all over the country, organized an army, and offered them training.

❸ After preparing for quite some time, Qiu Jin thought it was time they acted. Unfortunately, the secret leaked out and the government learned of their plan. Some leaders at another base were caught. Though her situation was critical, Qiu still had enough time to escape. Instead, she told her comrades: "No revolution can ever succeed without bloodshed!". She did not take their advice but waited to be caught at the base after the others had left. When the government soldiers arrived they took her away.

Though she was in their hands, Qiu did not yield to the government. Several days later, she was executed in public. She was only thirty-two years old when she died. She had always shown her strong faith in whatever she did. Before her execution she even wrote a poem to tell people that she did not regret anything. Her death made many people understand what the revolution meant to the country. After her death, more and more people joined the revolutionary force. Four years later, the revolution succeeded, and Qiu Jin's dream was realized.

Expansion Reading

Women's Liberation Movement in China

The women's liberation movement is a social campaign against sexual discrimination and in support of women's rights.

The equality of men and women is a condition that people use to judge how civilized a society is. It is also one of the most important objectives of the Chinese women's liberation movement. China had been a paternal society for many thousand years, and the status of women had always been low. They did not have the rights and chances to participate in politics, receive education, and enjoy the social life.

Of all the old customs, foot-binding was definitely the worst, cruelest one. It ruined women physically and mentally. It showed how women were treated disrespectfully in the past, but it was a standard for beauty in old society for almost 300 years. The girls' mothers would bind the feet of girls with cotton bandages until they became a tiny and pointed shape. During the whole process, the females had to suffer great pain.

Besides foot-binding, there were also the traditional doctrines like "Three Os", which specified what women should and should not do. "Three Os" asked the females to obey their fathers when they were maidens at home, obey their men after marriage, and obey their sons after the death of their husbands.

Chinese women fought for the right of education.

The Chinese women movement started in the early 20th century. In Shanghai books discussing women issues were found in bookshops, and then somebody chanted the slogan "Long Live Women

Rights". These were followed by legalization of women education, participation of women in politics, the first-ever divorce lawsuit filed by a woman and was accepted ...
To set the women free from the social restraints, many women got involved in the movements, and some even had given their lives. In their incessant endeavors, the social status of women has changed dramatically during the past decades. Nowadays, many more women have proactively participated in every aspect of national as well as social affairs.

GAMES FOR FUN

The last words of Qiu Jin were:

秋风秋雨愁煞人

Circle the characters related to Qiu Jin's name.

Answers: 秋风秋雨愁煞人

Jiù le xǔduō rén de jìnǚ

救了许多人的妓女——

Sài Jīnhuā

赛金花

Sai Jinhua — The Prostitute Who Saved Many People

Pre-reading Questions

1. What could a prostitute have done to become a “respectable” person?
2. Sai Jinhua had been a prostitute. What kind of difficulties do you think Sai Jinhua would have after her husband's death?

Zài Zhōngguó jìnǚ shì méiyǒu dìwèi de Dànshì zài

1 在中国，妓女是没有地位的。但是，在

yībǎiduō nián qián yǒu yī gè jìnǚ zài guójiā yǒu wēixiǎn

一百多年前，有一个妓女，在国家有危险

de shíhou jiùle hěnduō Zhōngguórén suǒyǐ hěn shòu rén

的时候，救了很多中国人，所以很受人

zūnjìng Tā jiùshì Sài Jīnhuā

尊敬。她就是赛金花。

Sài Jīnhuā de jiāli hěn qióng shísì suì de shíhou

赛金花的家里很穷，十四岁的时候，

tā bèi jiāli de rén mài le biànchéng jìnǚ Tā hěn

她被家里的人卖了，变成妓女。她很

cōngmíng rén yòu cháng de piàoliang hěnkuài jiù hóng qilai

聪明，人又长得漂亮，很快就红起来。

Yī nián hòu Sài Jīnhuā yùdào yī gè hěn yǒu qiántú de
一年后，赛金花遇到一个很有前途的

guānyuán Tā jiànle Sài Jīnhuā fēicháng xǐhuan tā hái
官员。他见了赛金花，非常喜欢她，还

jiāng tā qǔ huíjiā qù Bùjiǔ zhège guānyuán chéngle
将她娶回家去。不久，这个官员成了

wàijiāodàchén dàibiǎo Zhōngguó gēn Ōuzhōu jǐgè guójiā jiànlì
外交大臣，代表中国跟欧洲几个国家建立

guānxì Yúshì Sài Jīnhuā péi zhe zhàngfu zǒuchū Zhōngguó
关系。于是，赛金花陪着丈夫走出中国。

Tā gēn zhàngfu yīqǐ dàoguo hěnduō dàichéngshì hái jiànguo
她跟丈夫一起到过很多大城市，还见过

Déguó de huángdì Sài Jīnhuā bùgù zhàngfu de fǎnduì
德国的皇帝。赛金花不顾丈夫的反对，

nǔlì xuéxí Déyǔ hé tiàowǔ jiéguǒ tā zài Ōuzhōu dà
努力学习德语和跳舞，结果她在欧洲大

shòu huānyíng hái bèi chēngwéi dōngfāng zuì piàoliang de nǚrén
受欢迎，还被称为“东方最漂亮的女人”。

This is an ancient painting of Suzhou where Sai Jinhua was sold to be a prostitute.

Sān nián hòu Sài Jīnhuā yǔ zhàngfu huídào Zhōngguó Hěn
❷ 三年后，赛金花与丈夫回到中国。很
bùxìng tā de zhàngfu jǐnián hòu bìngsǐ le Yóuyú yǐqián
不幸，她的丈夫几年后病死了。由于以前
shì jìnǚ Sài Jīnhuā yīzhí bèi zhàngfu jiāli de rén
是妓女，赛金花一直被丈夫家里的人
kànbuqǐ zuìhòu zhǐhǎo líkāi Wèile shēnghuó niánqīng
看不起，最后只好离开。为了生活，年轻
de Sài Jīnhuā láidào Běijīng zài yīcì zuò jìnǚ
的赛金花来到北京，再一次做妓女。
Yījiǔlínglíng nián Zhōngguó gēn wàiguó dǎzhàng hěnkuài biàn bèi
一九〇〇年，中国跟外国打仗，很快便被
dǎbài Bā gè guójiā de liánhé jūnduì gōng rù Běijīng
打败。八个国家的联合军队攻入北京，
hái zhànlǐng le huángdì de gōngdiàn Huángdì táo dào Xī'ān
还占领了皇帝的宫殿。皇帝逃到西安，
liú xiàlái de lǎobǎixìng sǐ de sǐ shāng de shāng sìchù
留下来的老百姓死的死，伤的伤，四处
yīpiàn hùnluàn Dāngshí Sài Jīnhuā zhù de dìfang yóu Déguó
一片混乱。当时赛金花住的地方，由德国
de jūnduì guǎnlǐ Yǒu yī yè Déguó shìbīng chuǎngjìn Sài
的军队管理。有一夜，德国士兵闯进赛
Jīnhuā de jiā Sài Jīnhuā yòng liúlì de Déyǔ gēn tāmen
金花的家。赛金花用流利的德语跟他们
tánhuà hái náchū tā gēn Déguó huángdì de zhàopiàn gěi
谈话，还拿出她跟德国皇帝的照片给
tāmen kàn Zhèxiē shìbīng hěn jīngqí lòngbùqīng Sài Jīnhuā
他们看。这些士兵很惊奇，弄不清赛金花
de shēnfen zhǐhǎo líkāi
的身份，只好离开。
Dì-èr tiān Sài Jīnhuā bèi jiēdào huángdì de gōngdiàn
第二天，赛金花被接到皇帝的宫殿，

gēn liánhé jūnduì de zuìgāo jūnguān jiànmiàn Dāng Sài Jīnhuā
跟联合军队的最高军官见面。当赛金花

jìnrù gōngdiàn de shíhou tā gǎndào hěn nánguò Tā xiǎng
进入宫殿的时候，她感到很难过。她想：

Yī gè guójiā zuì zhòngyào de dìfang dōu bèi rén zhànlǐng le
“一个国家最重要的地方都被人占领了，

zhège guójiā de qiántú huì zěnyàng ne Tā juédìng yòng
这个国家的前途会怎样呢？”她决定用

zìjǐ wēixiǎo de lìliang bāngzhù zhège tā rè'ài de guójiā
自己微小的力量，帮助这个她热爱的国家。

3 Yóuyú Sài Jīnhuā de Déyǔ hěn liúlì shùnlì bāngzhù
由于赛金花的德语很流利，顺利帮助

jūnduì jiějué le liángshi wèntí hěnkuài biàn dédào zuìgāo
军队解决了粮食问题，很快便得到最高

jūnguān de xìnrèn Dāngshí wàiguó jūnduì zài Běijīng dàochù
军官的信任。当时，外国军队在北京到处

shārén Sài Jīnhuā kàn zài yǎnli fēicháng zháojí Dāng tā
杀人。赛金花看在眼里，非常着急。当她

gēn zuìgāo jūnguān jiànmiàn de shíhou duì tā shuō Nǐmen
跟最高军官见面的时候，对他说：“你们

A well-known prostitute in the late Qing dynasty.

de jūnduì lái zì wénmíng de guójiā zhòngshì jìlǜ shì
的军队来自文明的国家，重视纪律，是
bùhuì suíbiàn shārén de Yīnwèi zhè jù huà wàiguó
不会随便杀人的。”因为这句话，外国
jūnduì tíngzhǐ shānghài Zhōngguó de lǎobǎixìng wúshù rén
军队停止伤害中国的老百姓，无数人
yīncǐ bǎocún le shēngmìng Wèile ràng liánhé jūnduì kuàidiǎn
因此保存了生命。为了让联合军队快点
líkāi Zhōngguó guānyuán gēn tāmen jìnxíng le hétán
离开，中国官员跟他们进行了和谈。
Bùguò yī gè Déguó wàijiāodàchén bèi shā hétán yīncǐ
不过，一个德国外交大臣被杀，和谈因此
tíng xiàlai Zhōngguó guānyuán qǐngqiú Sài Jīnhuā bāngzhù tā
停下来。中国官员请求赛金花帮助，她
tíyì wèi sǐ le de Déguó dàchén zào yīzuò jìniàn bēi
提议为死了的德国大臣造一座纪念碑，
suànshì xiàng Déguó zhèngfǔ dàoqiàn Tā de jiànyì chénggōng
算是向德国政府道歉。她的建议成功
le wàiguó jūnduì zhōngyú líkāi Zhōngguó Lǎobǎixìng zhīdào
了，外国军队终于离开中国。老百姓知道
hòu fēicháng gǎnjī Sài Jīnhuā Suīrán zhīdào tā bù shì
后，非常感激赛金花。虽然知道她不是
guānyuán dàn dōu chēng tā wéi hétán dàchén
官员，但都称她为“和谈大臣”。

Wàiguó jūnduì líkāi de nà yī nián Sài Jīnhuā cái
外国军队离开的那一年，赛金花才
sānshí suì Tā réngrán huíqù zuò jìnǚ shēnghuó yīzhí
三十岁。她仍然回去做妓女，生活一直
hěn pínqióng Yóuyú tā rèxīn bāngzhù rén dàjiā hěn zūnjìng
很贫穷。由于她热心帮助人，大家很尊敬
tā tā de gùshi yě yīzhí liúchuán xiàlai
她，她的故事也一直流传下来。

Translation

❶ Like in many other countries, prostitutes in China are the people at the bottom of society. However, a hundred years ago, when China was in great danger, a woman had come out and saved many people's lives. This savior happened to be a prostitute, and her name was Sai Jinhua.

Sai Jinhua was born into a very poor family. When she was fourteen she was sold to a brothel. She was so clever and beautiful that she became very popular in no time. A year later she met a promising official. The man fell into love with her at first sight and married her immediately. Soon this official became a diplomatic official and representative of China in Europe. Sai Jinhua had a chance to step out of China accompanying her husband. The couple had been to many big cities, and had even met with the German emperor. Disregarding of her husband's objection, Sai Jinhua learned German and dancing. She became popular in Europe. "The most beautiful Asian woman" was the phrase that people there praised her.

❷ Three years later, Sai Jinhua came back to China with her husband. Unfortunately, her husband died of a serious illness several years after they had returned home. Because she was once a prostitute, her husband's family looked down upon her. At last, leaving home seemed her only choice. To make a living she went to Peking and became a prostitute again. In 1900 a war broke out between China and many foreign countries. China was defeated in just a few months. The Eight-Nation Alliance forced their way into Peking and even took over the Imperial Palace. The Emperor fled but left his people to suffer. A lot of people were injured and killed. Everywhere was in a chaos. Sai Jinhua was then living in an area under the rule of the German troop. One night some German soldiers broke into her home. Sai Jinhua not only talked to them in very fluent German, but also showed them photographs in which she posed with the German Emperor. The soldiers were amazed to see that. They wondered who this woman was, and they did not dare to make a fuss but left the house in awe.

The following day, Sai Jinhua was led to the palace to meet the commander-in-chief of the alliance troops. Sai Jinhua felt very sad while she was walking through the passages into the palace. "What will happen to this country while its most important place is being occupied by invaders?" She thought. She was determined to use all her power, though little, to help the country that she loved.

❸ The troops' problem of food shortage was pressing then. As Sai Jinhua spoke very fluent German and helped solve the problem, she won her the trust of the commander-in-chief. During that time the alliance troops in Peking were killing Chinese people deliberately. Sai Jinhua was very worried about it. "Your soldiers come from civilized countries. You see discipline a very important thing. You don't kill people for pleasure, do you?" said Sai, when she met the commander-in-chief. Because of what she had said, the foreign troops did not harm the Chinese people any more, and countless lives had thus been saved. To make the troops leave their country the Chinese officials went to discuss with them. But the negotiations came to a halt when a German diplomatic minister was killed. Chinese officials asked for her help, she suggested that they build a memorial for the dead minister as an apology to the German government. Her idea worked well, and the troops left China at last. When they heard the news, the Chinese people felt very grateful to her for what she had done. Although she had not hold an office, people still called her "Peacemaking Minister".

Sai Jinhua was only thirty when the alliance troops left Peking. She went back to her old job and had been living in poverty ever since. She was highly respected for what she had done for the country, and her story was told from generation to generation.

Expansion Reading

The Destruction of Yuan Ming Yuan

Many Chinese people were killed when the Eight-Nation Alliance entered Beijing. Because Sai Jinhua urged them not to kill anymore, the foreign soldiers stopped the killing, and thus many innocent lives were spared. However, Sai Jinhua was only a human being; she alone could not stop the troops of the eight countries from destroying Yuan Ming Yuan – the famous and largest imperial garden in China.

Yuan Ming Yuan is situated in present-day Beijing. It had involved five emperors and took over 150 years to finish, and it had cost a great deal of labour and money. The architecture itself was not only a magnificent palace, but the huge collection of art works that it held was also magnificent. However, the palace was razed to the ground by two disastrous destructions. The first destruction happened in 1860 when the Anglo-French troops entered Beijing, the soldiers looted Yuan Ming Yuan and taken away most of its cultural artifacts and valuables. As for those immovable expensive giant ceramic wares, they were smashed to pieces. After looting the soldiers set fire to the palace. The fire had lasted for three whole days, reducing most of the architecture to ashes.

The second disaster happened in 1900 when the Alliance troops invaded Beijing. The troops set fire to Yuan Ming Yuan again, destroying the remaining thirteen imperial buildings. Subsequently, the relics were stolen by the Chinese soldiers and profiteers again and again. Whenever there was a chance, people would move away stone sculptures and materials wholesale for their own gardens. Some precious rocks were also sold piece by piece. In the end, Yuan Ming Yuan had become complete ruins.

One can say that Yuan Ming Yuan was destroyed by the Anglo-French troops and the Eight-Nation Alliance, of course, but it is also fair to say that it was destroyed in the hand of an inept government. Yuan Ming Yuan has not been rebuilt ever since, and it has been lying in ruins as ever.

GAMES FOR FUN

In 1900, Eight-Nation allied militaries invaded Beijing. Four nations in the alliance have been given to you as follows. Write the remainder in Chinese.

美国　　德国　　沙俄　　奥匈帝国

____

____

____

____

____

____

Answers: 英国、意大利、法国、日本

Kělián de nǚ gēxīng

可怜的女歌星——

Zhōu Xuán

周璇

Zhou Xuan — The Golden Voice

Zhou Xuan's portrait.

Pre-reading Questions

1. Have you ever listened to any Mandarin pop songs?
2. Do you think it is hard to become a famous singer in China?

---

1 Zhōu Xuán shì Zhōngguó shàng shìjì sān sìshí niándài zuì hóng
周 璇 是 中国 上 世纪 三、四十 年代 最 红
de nǚ yǎnyuán hé gēxīng Zhídào jīntiān rénmen réngrán
的 女 演员 和 歌星。直到 今天，人们 仍然
jìde tā Měicì dāng rénmen tīngdào tā de shēngyīn
记得 她。每次，当 人们 听到 她 的 声音，
dōuhuì xiǎngqǐ tā kělián de gùshi
都会 想起 她 可怜 的 故事。

Zhōu Xuán zài yī gè pínkǔ de jiātíng chūshēng Shēng
周 璇 在 一 个 贫苦 的 家庭 出生。生
xiàlai bùjiǔ jiù bèi fùqīn pāoqì zài lùbiān hòulái
下来 不久，就 被 父亲 抛弃 在 路边，后来
bèi rén shōuyǎng Bā suì nànián Zhōu Xuán bèi sòng qù xué
被 人 收养。八 岁 那年，周 璇 被 送 去 学

biǎoyǎn Shí'èr suì de shíhou wèile shēnghuó tā cānjiā
表演。十二岁的时候，为了生活，她参加
le yī gè xiǎo biǎoyǎn tuán sìchù yǎnchū
了一个小表演团，四处演出。

Zài tuán li Zhōu Zuán měitiān dōu nǔlì de xuéxí
在团里，周璇每天都努力地学习。
Zhōu Xuán de shēngyīn hěn měi dàn Pǔtōnghuà shuō de bù
周璇的声音很美，但普通话说得不
biāozhǔn yǐngxiǎng le gēchàng Dàn tā bùkěn fàngqì tā qǐng
标准，影响了歌唱。但她不肯放弃，她请
Pǔtōnghuà jiǎng de hěn biāozhǔn de rén lái dāng lǎoshī yī
普通话讲得很标准的人来当老师，一
gè zì yī gè zì de gēn tā xué bù liàn hǎo jiù bù tíng
个字一个字地跟他学，不练好就不停
xiàlai Jiù zhèyàng píngzhe nǔlì tā jìnbù hěnkuài
下来。就这样，凭着努力，她进步很快。

❷ Zhōu Xuán de nǔlì zhōngyú yǒu le huíbào Yǒu yī cì
周璇的努力终于有了回报。有一次，
fùzé biǎoyǎn de rén tūrán bùnéng lái yóu Zhōu Xuán dàitì
负责表演的人突然不能来，由周璇代替
yǎnchū Biǎoyǎn qián bùshǎo rén dōu dānxīn tā de yǎnchū
演出。表演前，不少人都担心她的演出
bùgòu hǎo jiéguǒ Zhōu Xuán de biǎoyǎn shòudào guānzhòng rèliè
不够好，结果周璇的表演受到观众热烈
huānyíng zhǎngshēng hěn cháng shíjiān dōu bùnéng tíng xialai
欢迎，掌声很长时间都不能停下来。
Zhètiān yǐhòu tā de gēchàng shìyè tà chū chénggōng de
这天以后，她的歌唱事业踏出成功的
dì-yī bù Bùjiǔ Zhōu Xuán cānjiā yī gè dàxíng de
第一步。不久，周璇参加一个大型的
gēchàng bǐsài qǔdé yàjūn Yī shíjiān bàokān zázhì
歌唱比赛，取得亚军。一时间，报刊、杂志

dōu bàodǎo tā de xiāoxi xǐhuan tā de rén yě yuèláiyuè
都报导她的消息，喜欢她的人也越来越
duō
多。

Dāngshí Zhōngguó de diànyǐng hángyè gānggāng fāzhǎn
当时，中国的电影行业刚刚发展
qǐlái Yī cì ǒurán de jīhuì xià Zhōu Xuán jìnrù
起来。一次偶然的机会下，周璇进入
le diànyǐng quān Suīrán dì-yī cì pāi diànyǐng dàn tā
了电影圈。虽然第一次拍电影，但她
de biǎoyǎn hěn jīngcǎi hái dédào rénmen de chēngzàn Zài
的表演很精彩，还得到人们的称赞。在
suíhòu de èrshí duō niánjiān Zhōu Xuán pāile sìshí duō bù
随后的二十多年间，周璇拍了四十多部
diànyǐng lùle èrbǎi duō shǒu gēqǔ Tā dútè de shēngyīn
电影，录了二百多首歌曲。她独特的声音
chuánbiànle Zhōngguó tā yě chéngle rénrén dōu zhīdào de míng
传遍了中国，她也成了人人都知道的名
gēxīng
歌星。

3 Shìyè de chénggōng méiyǒu wèi tā de gǎnqíng dàilai hǎo de
事业的成功，没有为她的感情带来好的
yùnqi Tā jiéguo sān cì
运气。她结过三次
hūn dōu yǐ shībài jiéshù
婚，都以失败结束。
Zhōu Xuán de dì-yī rèn zhàngfu
周璇的第一任丈夫
shì jiāo tā pǔtōnghuà de
是教她普通话的
lǎoshī Tā duì Zhōu Xuán hěn
老师。他对周璇很

Zhou Xuan's album.

hǎo kěshì tā hěn bù mǎnyì jiéhūn hòu de shēnghuó
好，可是，他很不满意结婚后的生活
shòudào tài duō rén de zhùyì méiyǒu yīdiǎn zìyóu Hěnduō
受到太多人的注意，没有一点自由。很多
rén shuō tā huàihuà shǐ Zhōu Xuán duì zhàngfu shīqù le
人说他坏话，使周璇对丈夫失去了
xìnxīn Zhōngyú liǎng rén de máodùn yuèláiyuè shēn hūnyīn
信心。终于，两人的矛盾越来越深，婚姻
hěnkuài jiù jiéshù le
很快就结束了。

Zhōu Xuán hòulái de liǎng cì hūnyīn gèngjiā shībài
周璇后来的两次婚姻，更加失败。
Tā bùdàn bèi rén piàn le gǎnqíng hái bèi rén piàn zǒu dà
她不但被人骗了感情，还被人骗走大
bùfen de qián Xiǎngbudào yī gè hóng biàn Zhōngguó de
部分的钱。想不到，一个红遍中国的
míng nǚrén jìngrán méiyǒu xiǎngshòu guò měihǎo de àiqíng
名女人，竟然没有享受过美好的爱情。
Gǎnqíng shàng de dǎjī shǐ Zhōu Xuán huànshangle kěpà de
感情上的打击，使周璇患上了可怕的
jīngshénbìng Yóuyú tā de bìngqíng hěn bù wěndìng gōngzuò tíng
精神病。由于她的病情很不稳定，工作停
le xiàlái Zài shēngmìng de zuìhòu jǐnián li Zhōu Xuán
了下来。在生命的最后几年里，周璇
shòule hěnduō kǔ Zhīchí tā huó xiàqu de lǐyóu shì
受了很多苦。支持她活下去的理由，是
xiǎng gēn zìjǐ de qīnrén yīqǐ shēnghuó Zhōngyú péngyou
想跟自己的亲人一起生活。终于，朋友
bǎ tā mǔqīn zhǎo chulai dàn tā mǔqīn jìngrán bùkěn gēn
把她母亲找出来，但她母亲竟然不肯跟
tā jiànmiàn Kělián de Zhōu Xuán yīzhí zài yīyuàn děngzhe
她见面。可怜的周璇一直在医院等着，

zhídào sǐqù tā dōu méi jiànguo zìjǐ de qīnrén
直到死去，她都没见过自己的亲人。

Zhōu Xuán sǐqù de shíhou cái sānshíjiǔ suì. Tā
周璇死去的时候，才三十九岁。她

liúxia dòngrén de shēngyīn háiyǒu yī gè ràng rén nánguò de
留下动人的声音，还有一个让人难过的

gùshi
故事。

Translation

❶ Zhou Xuan was the most popular actress and singer in China during the 1930's and 40's. People still remember her today. Her unique voice arouses memories of her tragic story.

Zhou was born into a very poor family. Shortly after she was born, she was dumped by her father at the roadside, but was rescued and adopted by a family. When she was eight Zhou was sent to a school to learn singing.

Zhou studied hard and practiced her skills every day. She had a very beautiful voice but could not speak standard Mandarin. This defect affected her performance, but she did not give up. She hired a teacher who spoke with a perfect accent. She learned word by word, and would not stop until she was totally satisfied. She worked so hard that she quickly showed great improvement.

❷ Eventually her efforts proved worthwhile. Once when a singer failed to show up, Zhou was asked to replace her. Before she came on to the stage, many people were worried that she was not good enough, but Zhou's brilliant performance proved that their doubts were unnecessary. The audience liked her so much that their applause seemed unable to stop. This was a crucial step in Zhou's singing career. Soon Zhou entered an important singing contest and took second prize. All of a sudden, her name appeared in every newspaper and magazine, and her popularity grew tremendously.

At that time the movie industry was just in its early stages. The singer Zhou Xuan became an actress by chance. Though she had no experience, her first performance was great and won the audience's praises. In the following twenty years, Zhou made more than forty movies and recorded over two hundred songs. Her unique voice was heard all over China, and Zhou Xuan became a household name.

❸ Career success did not bring luck into her love life. Zhou had three serious relationships, but all ended in failure. Her first husband was her Mandarin teacher. He was not bad to Zhou, but he was not happy with the public attention on their personal lives after they were married. He wanted to have his freedom back. At the same time, Zhou lost faith in her husband as many people said bad things about him. In the end, they both fell out of love and their marriage was over.

Her two subsequent relationships were even worse. She was not only cheated of her love, but was also cheated out of her money. No one understood why such a celebrity could not enjoy a normal love life. For her these emotional blows were fatal, and she developed serious mental problems. Because of her unstable mental condition, she could no longer work. In her last years, she suffered a great deal. It was only her strong wish to live together with her family that gave her the will to live on. Finally her friends found her mother, yet tragically she refused to see her daughter. The pathetic Zhou waited and waited in the hospital but was unable to see her family when she took her last breath.

She died at the young age of thirty-nine. The legacy that she left to us includes a moving voice and a tragic story.

Death from Suicide — The Fallen Star

Talking about Zhou Xuan, one would naturally think of Ruan Lingyu, and vice versa. Both of them were the superstars of the same time. Though they died of different causes: one of illness, the other of drug overdose, they shared the same fate; they both died young, had a very successful career, were losers in love, and were destroyed by the failure of their marriage.

Ruan Lingyu was born in Shanghai in 1910. She was one of the most famous actresses in silent movies. She made her first movie at the age of 16, and she rose to fame by playing the flower girl in a movie when she was 20. Ruan was such a brilliant actress that she was dubbed the Chinese Ingrid Bergman. In her short life she had made 29 movies.

However, like Zhou Xuan, success in career did not bring her success in love. When she was 16 she was seduced by a playboy into living together with him, and she had to start to make a living by acting to satisfy his needs. She married a rich businessman after she had freed herself from the playboy. She was 23 this year. However, in the end she found that he was also a cheat who saw women as toys.

Two years after she had married, Ruan was involved in a painful, nasty love triangle with her former lover and present husband. The private matter was widely publicized, and in no time became the talk of the town. This made the young actress extremely frustrated. In her depression she killed herself by taking poison at home. She was not yet 26 when she died. Her famous last words are: "Gossip is a fearful thing."

Ruan Lingyu's portrait.

Ruan's story was made into a movie, and the role was played by the famous actress Maggie Cheung. The movie was made like a documentary, interweaving the original shots by Ruan with the new ones by Maggie Cheung. The movie also contains the interviews of some veteran moviemakers and of Maggie

Cheung herself. The movie is thought-provoking. It makes you think about the causes of Ruan's tragedy besides mere regrets. The movie has been a huge success, and with her excellent performance Maggie Cheung took the best actress crown in the Berlin International Movie Festival.

GAMES FOR FUN

Take a look at the movie posters and read the cast list. Find out the movie(s) in which Zhou Xuan played the leading role(s).

(a)

(b)

(c)

Answers: (c)

Jìnǚ huàjiā
妓女画家——
Pān Yùliáng
潘玉良

Pan Yuliang — The Prostitute Turned Painter

Pre-reading Questions

1. If a successful person had a dishonorable past, would you still think highly of him?
2. How do you handle other people's negative comments?

Pān Yùliáng shì Zhōngguó jìndài de zhùmíng nǚ huàjiā. Tā de
1 潘玉良是中国近代的著名女画家。她的
yīshēng shì yī gè zhuīqiú mèngxiǎng de gùshi.
一生是一个追求梦想的故事。

Pān Yùliáng de fùqīn hé mǔqīn hěn zǎo biàn sǐ le,
潘玉良的父亲和母亲很早便死了，
bā suì biàn gēn jiùjiu yīqǐ shēnghuó. Shísì suì de
八岁便跟舅舅一起生活。十四岁的
shíhou, jiùjiu wèile qián, tōutōu bǎ Pān Yùliáng mài qù
时候，舅舅为了钱，偷偷把潘玉良卖去
zuò jìnǚ.
做妓女。

Sān nián hòu, yī gè gāojí guānyuán láidào Pān Yùliáng
三年后，一个高级官员来到潘玉良

jūzhù de chéngshì gōngzuò dāngdì zhèngfǔ jǔbàn le yīchǎng
居住的城市工作，当地政府举办了一场

yànhuì lái yíngjiē tā Yànhuì shàng Pān Yùliáng chàng le
宴会来迎接他。宴会上，潘玉良唱了

liǎng shǒu gē tā de shēngyīn xīyǐn le zhège guānyuán Tā
两首歌，她的声音吸引了这个官员。他

hàoqí de xiǎng Tā kàn qǐlai hěn shāngxīn a Wèishénme
好奇地想：“她看起来很伤心啊！为什么

zhème niánqīng jiù dāng jìnǚ ne Yúshì tā gēn Pān
这么年轻就当妓女呢？”于是，他跟潘

Yùliáng liáo qǐlai zhīdào le tā de jīnglì hòu fēicháng
玉良聊起来，知道了她的经历后，非常

tóngqíng tā
同情她。

Dì-èr tiān Pān Yùliáng péi zhe guānyuán yóulǎn
第二天，潘玉良陪着官员游览

zhège chéngshì Liǎng rén yīqǐ dùguò yúkuài de yī tiān
这个城市。两人一起度过愉快的一天，

Pān Yliáng hái zài tā de shēnshang gǎnshòu dào zūnzhòng hé
潘玉良还在他的身上感受到尊重和

wēnnuǎn Zài huíjiā de lùshang Pān Yùliáng qǐngqiú tā bǎ
温暖。在回家的路上，潘玉良请求他把

tā liúzài shēnbiān ér guānyuán yě dāying le Bùjiǔ Pān
她留在身边，而官员也答应了。不久，潘

Yùliáng dédào le zìyóu hái gēn tā jiéhūn le
玉良得到了自由，还跟他结婚了。

2 Jiéhūn hòu Pān Yùliáng láidào Shànghǎi kāishǐ le xīn
结婚后，潘玉良来到上海，开始了新

shēnghuó Zài yīcì ǒurán de jīhuì xià Pān Yùliáng yùdào
生活。在一次偶然的机会下，潘玉良遇到

le yī gè fēicháng yōuxiù de měishù lǎoshī Tā hěn yòngxīn
了一个非常优秀的美术老师。他很用心

de jiāo tā huàhuà hái gǔlì tā jìnrù měishù xuéyuàn
地教她画画，还鼓励她进入美术学院。

Tā de kǎoshì chéngjì hěn hǎo dàn xuéxiào de lǎoshī jìngrán
她的考试成绩很好，但学校的老师竟然

yīnwèi tā dāng guò jìnǚ bùkěn shōu tā Zuìhòu zài
因为她当过妓女，不肯收她。最后，在

xiàozhǎng de bāngzhù xià Pān Yùliáng cái kěyǐ jìnrù xuéyuàn
校长的帮助下，潘玉良才可以进入学院

dúshū
读书。

Zài xuéyuàn Pān Yùliáng hěn yòngxīn de xuéxí huìhuà
在学院，潘玉良很用心地学习绘画。

Yǒu yīcì shàngkè de shíhou lǎoshī yāoqiú xuésheng huà yī
有一次上课的时候，老师要求学生画一

gè méiyǒu chuān yīfu de shàonǚ Pān Yùliáng liǎnhóng le
个没有穿衣服的少女。潘玉良脸红了，

zhídào kèchéng jiéshù shénme dōu méiyǒu huà xialai Lǎoshī
直到课程结束，什么都没有画下来。老师

pīpíng le tā tā hěn nánshòu Huídào sùshè hòu tā
批评了她，她很难受。回到宿舍后，她

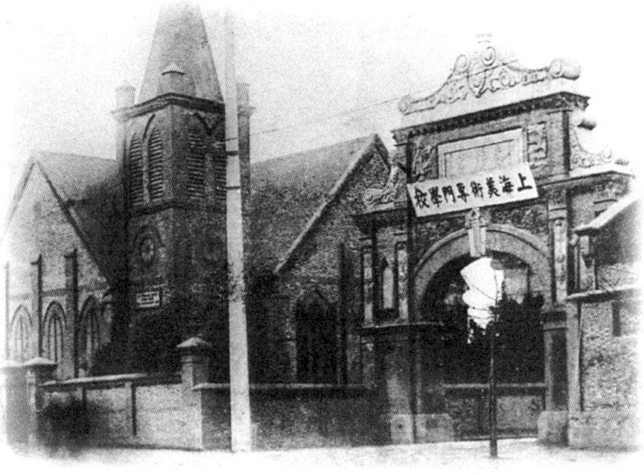

Shanghai Arts Academy.

xiǎng chū le yī gè bànfǎ Tā xiān bǎ ménchuāng guān hǎo
想出了一个办法。她先把门窗关好，

tuō qù shēnshang suǒyǒu de yīfu zuòzài jìngzi qián
脱去身上所有的衣服，坐在镜子前，

zǐxì de guānchá zìjǐ de shēntǐ ránhòu kāishǐ huìhuà
仔细地观察自己的身体，然后开始绘画。

Cóngcǐyǐhòu tā jīngcháng yòng zhège fāngfǎ lái liànxí
从此以后，她经常用这个方法来练习

huìhuà de jìqiǎo
绘画的技巧。

③ Sān nián hòu Pān Yùliáng yǐ dì-yī míng de chéngjì bìyè
三年后，潘玉良以第一名的成绩毕业。

Tā de réntǐ huà huà de hěn hǎo shǐ tā qǔdé dào wàiguó
她的人体画画得很好，使她取得到外国

xuéxí huìhuà de jīhuì Tā xiānhòu láidào Fǎguó hé
学习绘画的机会。她先后来到法国和

Yìdàlì jìnrù shìjiè wénmíng de měishù xuéyuàn xuéxí
意大利，进入世界闻名的美术学院学习。

Zhèduàn qījiān yóuyú zhàngfu shīqùle gōngzuò méiyǒu
这段期间，由于丈夫失去了工作，没有

jìqián gěi tā tā de shēnghuó hěn kǔ jīngcháng èzhe
寄钱给她，她的生活很苦，经常饿着

Paris in the early 20th century.

dùzi shàngkè yǒu yī cì hái zài kètáng shang yūndǎo
肚子上课，有一次还在课堂上晕倒。
Bùguò bùshǎo lǎoshī hé tóngxué dōu bāngzhù tā shǐ tā
不过，不少老师和同学都帮助她，使她
shùnlì wánchéng kèchéng
顺利完成课程。

Bìyè hòu Pān Yùliáng huídào Zhōngguó zài měishù
毕业后，潘玉良回到中国，在美术
xuéyuàn dāng lǎoshī Tā céngjīng wǔcì jǔbàn zuòpǐn zhǎnlǎn
学院当老师。她曾经五次举办作品展览，
dédào le hěn hǎo de chéngjì Bùguò tā de chénggōng
得到了很好的成绩。不过，她的成功
zhāolái hěnduō pīpíng Hěnduō rén yǐ tā dāngguo jìnǚ
招来很多批评。很多人以她当过妓女
de shì lái fǒudìng tā de chéngjiù ràng tā gǎndào shífēn
的事来否定她的成就，让她感到十分
nánguò Jǐnián hòu Zhōngguó fāshēng zhànzhēng wèile jìxù
难过。几年后，中国发生战争，为了继续
huà huà Pān Yùliáng rěnshòu gēn zhàngfu fēnlí de tòngkǔ
画画，潘玉良忍受跟丈夫分离的痛苦，
zài yī cì dào Fǎguó qù Zài Fǎguó tā chúle zuò
再一次到法国去。在法国，她除了做
yīxiē tuīdòng měishù de gōngzuò qíyú shíjiān dōu fàng
一些推动美术的工作，其余时间都放
zài huà shang Tā xiānhòu zài duō gè guójiā jǔbàn zuòpǐn
在画上。她先后在多个国家举办作品
zhǎnlǎn bìng zài jìngsài zhōng déjiǎng zhōngyú chéngwéile shìjiè
展览，并在竞赛中得奖，终于成为了世界
wénmíng de huàjiā
闻名的画家。

Translation

❶ Pan Yu-liang was a famous woman painter in the twentieth century. Her story tells how a woman pursued her dream.

Pan's parents died when she was still very young. From the time she was eight she lived with her uncle. When she was fourteen, her uncle sold her secretly to a brothel.

Three years later, a high-ranking government official came to the city where Pan lived, and the local government threw a banquet for him. At the banquet Pan sang two songs. The official was caught by her touching voice, and he thought: "She looks so sad! Why has she become a prostitute? She's just so young!" He was moved to speak with her. After hearing her pitiful story he felt great sympathy for her.

The following day, Pan accompanied the official visiting the city and they had a happy day. Pan felt his respect and concern. On their way home, Pan asked him if she could stay with him and the man agreed. Not long after, Pan got back her freedom and married him.

❷ After they were married, Pan moved to another city and began a new life. By chance she met a brilliant art teacher. He taught her with all his heart and encouraged her to go to an art academy. Her results in the entrance examination were very good, but the teachers there did not accept her because she was once a prostitute. In the end, with the help of the headmaster, Pan became a student of the academy.

Pan worked very hard at school. Once the teacher asked the class to draw a nude girl. Pan blushed and could not draw a line until the end of the lesson. The teacher criticized her, and Pan felt bad. When she went back to her dormitory, she found a way to solve her problem. First she closed the windows, locked the door, took all her clothes off and sat in front of a mirror. Then she looked at her own body carefully and began to draw. From then on, that was the way she practiced her drawing skills.

❸ Three years later, Pan graduated at the top of her class. Her nude pictures were exceptionally good and won her a scholarship to go abroad to study painting. She visited France and Italy and studied at world famous art academies. During that period, her husband lost his job. Without his money her life in Europe was hard. Often she went to class with an empty stomach, and once she fainted in the class. Luckily, many of her teachers and classmates gave her a hand, and she was able to finish her studies.

After graduation Pan came back to China and became a teacher at an art academy. She held art exhibitions five times and all of them were well received. However, her success also earned her jealous criticism. She was deeply upset as many people still attacked her for her dishonorable past and were not willing to recognize her achievements. Some years later, war broke out in China. Although it pained her, in order to continue to paint, Pan left her beloved husband and returned to France. There, she spent most of her time painting while doing art promotion work. She held exhibitions in many countries and won awards in competitions. Eventually she achieved the status of a world famous painter.

Expansion Reading

Xu Beihong — The Pioneer Artist

Pan Yu Lin is regarded as a first-rate painter of Western media in China, but she was not the only one who could combine traditional Chinese brushwork and the Western techniques. Xu Beihong, a classmate of Pan when they were in France, was also a prominent artist using the same method as Pan's. His accomplishment was unequalled at that time.

Xu was a great painter, art educator, and a founder of modern art education of China. He was born into a poor family, and began to learn painting from his father when he was a child. He taught art at school when he was 17 as a way to support his study at the university. He later traveled to Japan and France to study art. At the age of 28 he entered the distinguished national school of fine arts in Paris, where he studies oil-painting and drawing, and met classmate Pan Yu Lin. During that period he traveled around Europe, seeing and studying the arts there.

Xu came back to China and started his career as an art teacher when he was 32. From then on he held many exhibitions in many countries: France, Belgium, Italy, and so on, showing his own paintings or Chinese paintings by others. He loved his country dearly, so when the Anti-Japanese War broke out, he traveled to Hong Kong, Singapore, and India to hold exhibitions to raise money, and the money that he collected was given to rally supporters and the propaganda of fighting against Japan.

Xu's paintings show his mastery of combining various techniques: traditional, modern, Chinese and Western. His remarkable artistic talent and knowledge had broken a new ground for Chinese art. He excelled at drawing, oil-painting and Chinese painting. He also tried his hand on various motifs: landscape, bird-and-flower, animal, figure, historical, ... almost anything you can say. His galloping horse is world famous and has almost become the landmark of modern Chinese painting.

GAMES FOR FUN

Which of the following is Pan Yuliang's painting?

(a)

(b)

(c)

Answers: (b)

Zhōngguó Dì-yī fūrén

中国第一夫人——

Sòng Qìnglíng hé Sòng Měilíng

宋庆龄和宋美龄

The First Ladies of China — Song Qingling and Song Meiling

Pre-reading Questions

1. Do you think a woman could become successful much easier with her husband's help?
2. What would you do when you are on bad terms with your brothers and sisters?

Zài shàng shìjì chū, yǒu liǎng jiěmèi xiānhòu chéngwéi dì-yī
❶ 在上世纪初，有两姐妹先后成为第一
fūrén, tāmen de yīshēng dōu gēn Zhōngguó de mìngyùn lián zài
夫人，她们的一生都跟中国的命运连在
yīqǐ.
一起。

Sòng Qìnglíng hé Sòng Měilíng zài yī gè shāngrén de
宋庆龄和宋美龄在一个商人的
jiātíng chūshēng. Fùqīn hěn zhòngshì jiàoyù, hěn zǎo biàn bǎ
家庭出生。父亲很重视教育，很早便把
liǎng rén sòngwǎng Měiguó dúshū, xuéxí xīn sīxiǎng. Měiguó de
两人送往美国读书，学习新思想。美国的
jiàoyù, shǐ liǎng jiěmèi bǐ dāngshí de yībān fùnǚ dǒngde
教育，使两姐妹比当时的一般妇女懂得

gèng duō gèng guānxīn guójiā de qiántú Sòng Měilíng jiù céngjīng
更多，更关心国家的前途。宋美龄就曾经

zìháo de shuō guò Zhǐyǒu wǒ de liǎn xiàng gè Zhōngguórén
自豪地说过：“只有我的脸像个中国人！”

Tāmen liǎng rén dōu hěn yǒu cáinéng xìnggé què wánquán
她们两人都很有才能，性格却完全

bùtóng Sòng Qìnglíng hěn ài jìng jīngcháng yī gè rén liúzài
不同。宋庆龄很爱静，经常一个人留在

jiāli dúshū Sòng Měilíng xǐhuan rènao shēnbiān jīngcháng wéi
家里读书；宋美龄喜欢热闹，身边经常围

zhe péngyou Yóuyú Sòng Měilíng niánjì zuì xiǎo Sòng Qìnglíng
着朋友。由于宋美龄年纪最小，宋庆龄

zǒng ràng zhe tā shǐde Sòng Měilíng hěn rènxìng liǎng jiěmèi
总让着她，使得宋美龄很任性。两姐妹

xìnggé shàng de fēnbié shǐ tāmen hòulái zǒushàng le liǎng
性格上的分别，使她们后来走上了两

tiáo bùtóng de lù
条不同的路。

The museum of Song Qingling.

Sòng Qìnglíng de
❷ 宋庆龄的
zhàngfu shì jiéshù le huángdì
丈夫是结束了皇帝
tǒngzhì de gémìngjiā Sūn
统治的革命家孙
Zhōngshān Tā shì Sòng Qìnglíng
中山。他是宋庆龄
fùqīn de hǎo péngyou
父亲的好朋友，
bǐ tā niánzhǎng èrshí duō
比她年长二十多
suì Sòng Qìnglíng cóng Měiguó
岁。宋庆龄从美国
bìyè huílai hòu jiù dāng le Sūn Zhōngshān de zhùshǒu Nà
毕业回来后，就当了孙中山的助手。那
shíhou Sūn Zhōngshān suīrán zuò guò zǒngtǒng dànshì yǐjing
时候，孙中山虽然做过总统，但是已经
shīqù quánlì Sòng Qìnglíng bùgù jiāli de rén fǎnduì jià
失去权力。宋庆龄不顾家里的人反对嫁
gěi tā Shí nián hòu Sūn Zhōngshān bìngsǐ Wèile wánchéng
给他。十年后，孙中山病死。为了完成
zhàngfu sǐ qián zhuīqiú hépíng jiù Zhōngguó de yuànwàng Sòng
丈夫死前追求和平、救中国的愿望，宋
Qìnglíng zhīchí Gòngchǎndǎng Hòulái tā yīzhí yǐ pǔtōngrén
庆龄支持共产党。后来，她一直以普通人
de shēnfen lái zhīchí Zhōngguó de Gòngchǎnzhǔyì gémìng Tā de
的身份来支持中国的共产主义革命。她的
zuòfǎ dédào rénmen de zūnjìng hé kěndìng
做法，得到人们的尊敬和肯定。

Song Qingling and her husband Sun Yat-sen.

Xiāngduì lái shuō Sòng Měilíng gèng xǐ'ài zhèngzhì Tā zài
相对来说，宋美龄更喜爱政治。她在

yījiǔèrqī nián chéngwéi dì-yīfūrén

一九二七年 成为 第一夫人

hòu biàn kāishǐ zài duō fāngmiàn

后，便 开始 在 多 方面

bāngzhù zhàngfu Duì Sòng Měilíng lái

帮助 丈夫。对 宋 美龄 来

shuō jiéhūn shì yī gè fāhuī

说，结婚 是 一 个 发挥

cáinéng de jīhuì Tā de wàijiāo

才能 的 机会。她 的 外交

nénglì hěn qiáng gēn gè guó de

能力 很 强，跟 各 国 的

The front cover photo of Song Meiling on the January 1939 issue of *Click* magazine.

lǐngxiù jiànlìle liánghǎo de guānxì Zài Zhōngguó yǔ Rìběn

领袖 建立了 良好 的 关系。在 中国 与 日本

dǎzhàng qījiān tā zài Měiguó chénggōng de qǔdé Měiguórén

打仗 期间，她 在 美国 成功 地 取得 美国人

de zhīchí hé tóngqíng hái yǐnqǐ Sòng Měilíng rè

的 支持 和 同情，还 引起“宋 美龄 热”。

Hòulái zài Měiguó de bāngzhù xià wèi zhànzhēng de shènglì

后来 在 美国 的 帮助 下，为 战争 的 胜利

tígōngle jùdà bāngzhù

提供了 巨大 帮助。

Sòng Qìnglíng hé Sòng Měilíng zài guójì shang dōu hěn yǒumíng

3 宋 庆龄 和 宋 美龄 在 国际 上 都 很 有名，

dàn gěi rén de yìnxiàng wánquán bùtóng Sòng Qìnglíng de

但 给 人 的 印象 完全 不同。宋 庆龄 的

zhìhuì ràng jiànguo tā de wàiguórén liúxia hěn shēn de

智慧，让 见过 她 的 外国人 留下 很 深 的

yìnxiàng Sòng Měilíng duì guójì shìwù hěn yǒu xiǎngfǎ

印象。宋 美龄 对 国际 事务 很 有 想法，

jīngcháng fābiǎo pīpíng Tā shíyī cì chéngwéi Shídài

经常 发表 批评。她 十一 次 成为《时代》

Zázhì de fēngmiàn rénwù Hěnduō wàiguó lǐngxiù dōu gōngkāi
杂志 的 封面 人物。很多 外国 领袖 都 公开

shuō Sòng Měilíng shì zuì yǒu nénglì de nǚrén
说，宋 美龄 是“最 有 能力 的 女人”。

zài guónèi liǎng rén de zhèngzhì guāndiǎn chābié hěn
在 国内，两 人 的 政治 观点 差别 很

dà zhīchí de zhèngdǎng yě bù yīyàng Hòulái liǎng gè
大，支持 的 政党 也 不 一样。后来，两 个

zhèngdǎng yóu hézuò biànchéng duìlì shènzhì yīncǐ fāshēng
政党 由 合作 变成 对立，甚至 因此 发生

zhànzhēng guójiā chūxiàn fēnliè Cóngcǐ liǎng rén fēnbié
战争，国家 出现 分裂。从此，两 人 分别

le yīshēng méiyǒu zài jiànmiàn Zài Sòng Qìnglíng sǐ qián tā
了，一生 没有 再 见面。在 宋 庆龄 死 前，她

hěn xiǎng gēn mèimei jiànmiàn dàn Sòng Měilíng méiyǒu dāying
很 想 跟 妹妹 见面，但 宋 美龄 没有 答应。

Zhè liǎng gè nǚrén yīshēng dōu bù píngfán Tāmen
这 两 个 女人，一生 都 不 平凡。她们

gǎibiànle Zhōngguó gǎibiànle wàiguórén duì Zhōngguó nǚrén
改变了 中国，改变了 外国人 对 中国 女人

de kànfǎ Rénmen
的 看法。人们

dōu xǐhuan shuō Tāmen
都 喜欢 说：她们

yī gè ài guójiā
一 个 爱 国家，

yī gè ài quánlì
一 个 爱 权力。

Nǐ zěnyàng kàn ne
你 怎样 看 呢？

Song Meiling and Eleanor Roosevelt in 1943.

Translation

❶ Early last century, one by one two sisters became the first ladies of their country. Their lives were closely linked to the fate of China. They were the famous Song sisters.

Song Qingling and Song Meiling were born into a businessman's family. Their father thought highly of education so he sent his young daughters to America to study. He hoped that there they would learn modern thinking. Their American education taught them much more than the average women in China learned, and they came to care more about the future of their country. Meiling once proudly said: "I only look Chinese.!"

Both of them were talented, but their characters were totally different. Qingling enjoyed peace and quiet, and liked to study alone at home; Meiling loved meeting new people and enjoyed the company of friends. As Meiling was the youngest, Qingling always let her have her own way. That made Meiling a very headstrong girl. In the end, their different characters led them through two different paths in life.

❷ Qingling's husband was Dr. Sun Yat-sen, the revolutionary who overturned the imperial system. Dr. Sun was a good friend of Qingling's father, and was twenty-six years older than she. Qingling became Sun's secretary when she returned to China after graduation. Though he was president, Sun had already lost his political power. Nevertheless, Qingling married him, disregarding her family's objection. Ten years later, Sun died of cancer. To realize her husband's wish "Save China. Fight for Peace", Qingling began to support the Communist Party. In the following years, she kept on supporting the Communist revolution in China as an ordinary citizen. All that she did was good for the country, and won her the respect and recognition of the people.

Compared to her sister, Meiling was more interested in politics. When she became the first lady in 1927, she began to help her husband in many aspects. To Meiling, marriage was an opportunity for her to show her talent. Diplomacy was her specialty, and she established good relationships with the leaders of many countries. During the Anti-Japanese War, her excellent lobbying earned the support and sympathy of the American people for her country. She even stirred up a wave of popularity herself among the people during her visit to America. With the help of the American government, she laid the foundation of winning the war.

❸ Both Qingling and Meiling were world famous figures, but the impressions that they gave people were totally different. The foreigners who met Qingling were all impressed by her wisdom. Meiling had her own views on international affairs, and she often expressed them openly. She was on the cover of TIME magazine eleven times. Leaders of many countries said she was "the ablest woman that I've ever seen".

However, in China, the relationship between the two sisters grew tense. Not only the gap between their political views widened, but the parties that they supported were also different. Inevitably, the two collaborating parties came to oppose one another. To make things even worse, civil war broke out and the country split up. Therefore, the sisters bade farewell, and for the rest of their lives they never met again. On her deathbed Qingling expressed her wish to see her young sister, but Meiling did not come to her side.

Both of them were extraordinary women. They not only changed the fate of China, but also changed the impressions foreigners had of Chinese women. People would say: one of them loved the country while the other loved power. What do you think?

The First Ladies of China in Power

Besides the famous Qingling and Meiling, the Song family had another daughter, Ailing, who was an equally influential figure of the time, if not that famous as her two younger sisters. Ailing was the eldest of the children, and she was the one that her father had the greatest expectation for. He wished to make her a role model for her siblings. Like her two sisters, Ailing was remarkably beautiful and intelligent. She was especially good at money management, and she had an exceptionally strong desire for money. Because of her keen interest in making money she chose a different path in life – marrying to a famous banker and successful businessman, and becoming an extremely rich person by using her husband's social status and inside information of the financial market.

The movie "The Song Sisters" by Hong Kong director Mabel Cheung is a portrayal of the three sisters. Ailing, Qingling and Meiling are played by famous actresses Michelle Yeoh, Maggie Cheung and Vivian Wu respectively. "Long ago, in old China, there were three sisters; the first one loved money, the second her country, the third power." This first-ever line of the movie has become so popular that it is now the most famous comment about them. The movie uses their love lives as the main thread. It tells the relationship between the two splits of the family and the revolution in China. The sisters' relation is thick, and they had deep love for each other, but yet they are forced to go separate ways because of their different views on politics. They cannot even pour their hearts out when they meet up. The story is subtly narrated from the viewpoint of a female director. With the excellent performances of the three actresses the movie has been a great success and become a classic.

GAMES FOR FUN

Identify the lady standing next to Sun Yat-sen.

Answers: 宋庆龄

Zhōngguó dāngdài nǚ yǎnyuán

中国当代女演员——

Zhāng Mànyù Gǒng Lì Yáng Zǐqióng

张曼玉、巩俐、杨紫琼

Maggie Cheung, Gong Li and Michelle Yeoh — Chinese Actresses of Today

Pre-reading Questions

1. Who is your favorite Chinese actress?
2. What qualities do you think an excellent actress should have ?

---

❶ Nǐ kànguo Zhōngguó diànyǐng ma Yǒu méiyǒu tīngguo Zhāng
你看过中国电影吗？有没有听过张
Mànyù Gǒng Lì Yáng Zǐqióng zhèxiē míngzi Tāmen shì
曼玉、巩俐、杨紫琼这些名字？她们是
Zhōngguó dāngdài zuì zhùmíng de nǚ yǎnyuán Měicì chūxiàn de
中国当代最著名的女演员。每次出现的
shíhou dōu shòudào rénmen de mìqiè zhùyì
时候，都受到人们的密切注意。

Sān rén dāngzhōng chúle Zhāng Mànyù wài Gǒng Lì
三人当中，除了张曼玉外，巩俐
hé Yáng Zǐqióng dōu céng xuéxí biǎoyǎn Zhāng Mànyù zuìxiān
和杨紫琼都曾学习表演。张曼玉最先
pāi guǎnggào hòulái tōngguò xuǎnměi bǐsài jìnrù diànyǐng
拍广告，后来通过选美比赛进入电影
quān Tā zǎoqī pāile dàliàng diànyǐng biǎoxiàn hěn yībān
圈。她早期拍了大量电影，表现很一般。

Yǒuxiē rén shènzhì rènwéi tā de diànyǐng shēngmìng bùhuì tài
有些 人 甚至 认为，她 的 电影 生命 不会 太

cháng Bùguò dàliàng de yǎnchū jīngyàn shǐ tā de jìnbù
长。不过，大量 的 演出 经验 使 她 的 进步

yùláiyù dà zhújiàn chéngwéi dǎoyǎn zuì xǐ'ài de nǚ
愈来愈 大，逐渐 成为 导演 最 喜爱 的 女

yǎnyuán
演员。

Gǒng Lì zài dúshū de shíhou jiù bèi dǎoyǎn kànzhòng
巩 俐 在 读书 的 时候 就 被 导演 看中，

dānrèn nǚzhǔjué Jìnrù diànyǐng quān de qiánjǐ nián tā pāi
担任 女主角。进入 电影 圈 的 前几 年，她 拍

de diànyǐng bù duō dàn měi yī bù dōu hěn chénggōng Tā
的 电影 不 多，但 每 一 部 都 很 成功。她

de zhuānyè yǎnchū gèng dédào yīzhì de hǎopíng
的 专业 演出，更 得到 一致 的 好评。

Yáng Zǐqióng yě shì tōngguò xuǎnměi bǐsài jìnrù diànyǐng
杨 紫琼 也 是 通过 选美 比赛 进入 电影

quān de Gēn Zhāng Mànyù hé Gǒng Lì bùtóng de shì
圈 的。跟 张 曼玉 和 巩 俐 不同 的 是，

tā yīzhí zài dòngzuò yǎnchū shang fāzhǎn Tā dǒngde zhēn
她 一直 在 动作 演出 上 发展。她 懂得 真

gōngfu jīngcháng biǎoyǎn wēixiǎn dòngzuò Duì hěnduō guānzhòng
功夫，经常 表演 危险 动作。对 很多 观众

lái shuō Yáng Zǐqióng de dòngzuò yǎnchū shì hěn yǒu xīnshǎng
来 说，杨 紫琼 的 动作 演出，是 很 有 欣赏

jiàzhí de
价值 的。

Zài diànyǐng quān yào chénggōng chúle yùnqi gèng xūyào
❷ 在 电影 圈，要 成功，除了 运气，更 需要

nǔlì Tāmen sān rén dōu shì hǎo yǎnyuán pāishè de shíhou
努力。她们 三 人 都 是 好 演员，拍摄 的 时候

hěn rènzhēn yě méiyǒu jiàzi Wèile yǎnchū chénggōng dōu
很认真，也没有架子。为了演出成功，都

kěn huā dàliàng shíjiān zuò zhǔnbèi
肯花大量时间做准备。

Zhāng Mànyù néng yǎn rènhé diànyǐng rénwù tā de
张曼玉能演任何电影人物，她的

xíngxiàng biànhuà hěn dà lìng rén jīngqí Gǒng Lì de yǎnchū
形象变化很大，令人惊奇。巩俐的演出

hěn zhēnshí yī gè wàiguó míng dǎoyǎn shuō tā shì nàzhǒng
很真实，一个外国名导演说她是那种

Tīngbùdǒng tā shuō shénme dōu zhīdào tā zài yǎn shénme
“听不懂她说什么，都知道她在演什么”

de hǎo yǎnyuán Liǎng rén de biǎoyǎn nénglì chúle dédào
的好演员。两人的表演能力，除了得到

shìjiè gè dì guānzhòng de zhǎngshēng yě dédào zhuānyè
世界各地观众的掌声，也得到专业

rényuán de kěndìng Tāmen xiānhòu zài shìjiè sān dà guójì
人员的肯定。她们先后在世界三大国际

diànyǐngjié zhōng qǔdé zuì yōuxiù nǚ yǎnyuán jiǎng hòulái gèng
电影节中取得最优秀女演员奖，后来更

chéngwéi zhèxiē guójì diànyǐngjié de jìngsài píngshěn wěiyuán
成为这些国际电影节的竞赛评审委员。

Zhāng Mànyù hé Gǒng Lì de chéngjiù dào mùqián réngrán
张曼玉和巩俐的成就，到目前仍然

Maggie Cheung's palm print at the Star Avenue in Hong Kong.

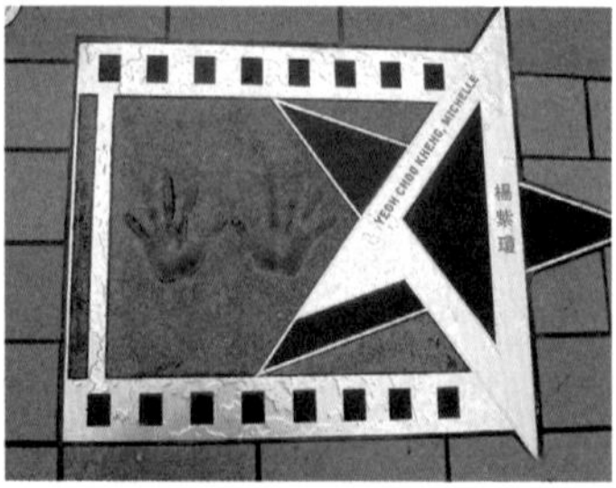

Michelle Yeoh's palm print at the Star Avenue in Hong Kong.

Maggie Cheung.

Michelle Yeoh.

méiyǒu rén nénggòu chāoguò
没有 人 能够 超过。

Zhìyú Yáng Zǐqióng tā shì Yàzhōu pái zài dì-yī wèi
至于 杨 紫琼，她 是 亚洲 排 在 第一 位

de dòngzuò nǔ yǎnyuán Jīngcǎi de dòngzuò yǎnchū shǐ tā
的 动作 女 演员。精彩 的 动作 演出，使 她

dédào hěnduō rén de zūnzhòng jīngcháng bèi yāoqǐng chūxí
得到 很多 人 的 尊重，经常 被 邀请 出席

gègè diànyǐng diǎnlǐ
各个 电影 典礼。

Zài Zhōngguó yǎnyuán qǔdé chénggōng hòu dōuhuì xuǎnzé
❸ 在 中国，演员 取得 成功 后，都会 选择

jìnrù guójì diànyǐng quān jiēshòu kǎoyàn
进入 国际 电影 圈，接受 考验。

Zhāng Mànyù céng zài duō bù Ōuzhōu diànyǐng dānrèn nǔ
张 曼玉 曾 在 多 部 欧洲 电影 担任 女

zhǔjué hòulái hái jià gěi yī gè Ōuzhōu dǎoyǎn Suīrán
主角，后来 还 嫁 给 一 个 欧洲 导演。虽然

zhèduàn hūnyīn hěnkuài jiù jiéshù le xiànzài de Zhāng Mànyù
这段 婚姻 很快 就 结束 了，现在 的 张 曼玉

réngrán shì yóuzǒu zài Yàzhōu yǔ Ōuzhōu zhījiān de guójì nǚ
仍然是游走在亚洲与欧洲之间的国际女

yǎnyuán
演员。

Gong Li.

Gǒng Lì yǔ Yáng Zǐqióng jiù
巩俐与杨紫琼就

xuǎnzé zài Hélǐhuó fāzhǎn
选择在荷里活发展。

Gǒng Lì pāiguo jǐ bù diànyǐng
巩俐拍过几部电影，

chéngjì yībān Yáng Zǐqióng céng
成绩一般。杨紫琼曾

pāishè Línglíngqī diànyǐng yǎn
拍摄零零七电影，演

yī gè gōngfu hěn hǎo de Zhōngguó
一个功夫很好的中国

nǚ tèwù Tā zài diànyǐng zhōng de dòngzuò yǎnchū ràng
女特务。她在电影中的动作演出，让

tā hěnkuài zài Hélǐhuó hóng qǐlai hòulái hái chéngwéi
她很快在荷里活红起来，后来还成为

Aosīkǎjiǎng de wěiyuán
奥斯卡奖的委员。

mùqián Zhōngguó diànyǐng réng zài gāosù fāzhǎn zhōng
目前，中国电影仍在高速发展中。

Xiāngxìn zài wèilái jǐ nián jiāng yǒu gèng duō nǚ yǎnyuán zǒuchū
相信在未来几年，将有更多女演员走出

Zhōngguó ràng nǐ kàndào tāmen de jīngcǎi yǎnchū
中国，让你看到她们的精彩演出。

Translation

❶ If you have you seen any Chinese movies, you will have heard the names of Maggie Cheung, Gong Li and Michelle Yeoh. They are the most popular Chinese actresses of today. Every time they appear in public they become the centre of attention.

Gong Li and Michelle Yeoh studied acting while Maggie's first performance was to make a TV advertisement. Then she entered a beauty pageant and later became an actress. In her early days in the industry she made many movies, but her performances did not leave an impression. Some people even thought that she would not stay long in the movie industry. Nevertheless, her acting was much improved as she became more and more experienced, and she gradually became the directors' favorite.

Gong Li was picked by the director to be the heroine in his movie when she was still a student. She did not make many movies in her first years as an actress, but every time she did it was a success. Her acting and professionalism have earned her the praise of all.

Like Maggie, Michelle also entered the industry through a beauty pageant. But what makes her different from Maggie and Gong Li is that she primarily makes action movies. Her kung fu is genuine, and she often carries out dangerous stunts by herself. Many audiences find Michelle's performances to be highly entertaining.

❷ Hard work and luck always go hand in hand in the movie industry. The three women are all great actresses. Whenever and wherever they work, they are very serious, yet they are friendly to fans and the people they work with. To give their best in their movies they put a lot of time and effort in preparation.

Maggie is a versatile actress, and she has created many different roles, which are all amazing. Gong Li's approach is down-to-earth. "You know what she's acting even though you don't understand what she says", a famous foreign director once said about her. Their abilities have not only won the applause of the worldwide audience, but have also been recognized by their fellow professionals. Both of them have won best actress awards in three major movie festivals, and have been appointed festival selection committee members . Their achievements have not yet been surpassed.

As for Michelle, she is regarded as the best action actress in Asia. She has earned everybody's respect with her impeccable stunts. She is often invited to attend various movie ceremonies.

❸ In China, it is common practice for actors to work internationally, to take on further challenges after they have become leading actors at home.

Maggie has played leading roles in many European movies. She even married a European director, although their marriage did not last. Maggie is still an active actress in both Asia and Europe.

Gong Li and Michelle have chosen to develop their careers in Hollywood. Gong Li has made several movies but has yet to make a hit. Michelle was once a Bond girl. In the 007 movie she plays a spy from China with excellent Kung fu. Her action talent has made her popular in Hollywood and she is a committee member of the Academy Awards.

The movie industry in China is developing at a fast pace. It is believed that more and more actresses will emerge from China, for a worldwide audience to enjoy.

Major Chinese Movie Awards

More and more Chinese actresses have gone international these years. Those who can show their glamour on the international stage are all well experienced and talented. Before they start to develop their career elsewhere they have to get the recognition of their acting by their peers in China proper. How well they are received can be represented by the awards they get. So what are the awards in the Chinese regions?

There are three most important awards, i.e. the Hong Kong Movie Awards of Hong Kong, the Golden Rooster Awards and the People's Hundred Flowers Awards of mainland China, and the Golden Horse Movie Awards of Taiwan.

The Hong Kong Movie Awards was set up in 1982 at a time when the movie industry in Hong Kong was flourishing. The establishment of the Awards had encouraged the moviemakers in a big way. The Awards are the "Oscar" to many movie people, and the festival is also the most important platform and activity for them to show their works and share their views.

The Golden Rooster Awards and the Hundred Flowers Awards are called the Dual Chinese Movie Awards. The Golden Rooster Awards are the most important awards among all in China, and winners are selected by a jury of movie professionals, so they are also called "the Experts' Awards". The first Golden Awards were held in 1981 by China Movie Association to encourage people to make quality movies and honor those who had got excellent results. The Hundred Flowers Awards was first organized by *Popular Cinema*, the best selling magazine in China, in 1962. Their results reflect the opinions and taste of the general cinema-goers, so they are called "the Audience Awards".

The Golden Horse Awards were set up in 1962, and are now sponsored by the Motion Picture Development Foundation of the R.O.C. The awards ceremony is held annually for all the movies made in the Chinese language.

As mentioned in the previous article, some actresses have won a lot of awards in the Chinese Movie festivals. Maggie Cheung has won many times in the Hong Kong Movie Awards and Golden Horse Movie Awards, and Gong Li, besides a couple of wins in the Dual

Awards, has made some movies that entered the top ten list of the Hong Kong Movie Awards.

GAMES FOR FUN

Circle the Chinese names of famous actresses.

黄一山	舒　琪	吴念祖	任达华
范冰冰	吴　京	胡　军	章子怡

Answers: 黄一山　(舒　琪)　吴念祖　任达华
(范冰冰)　吴　京　胡　军　(章子怡)

Glossary

Common Words and Phrases			HSK Rank	Page
bùgù	不顾	disregard	E/I	57
bùmǎn	不满	dissatisfaction	E/I	14
cāngbái	苍白	pale	E/I	26
chīkǔ	吃苦	suffer	E/I	03
dàchén	大臣	minister	Adv	12
dǎzhàng	打仗	at war	E/I	02
dútè	独特	unique	E/I	13
fǎngzhī	纺织	weaving fabrics	E/I	25
fùyù	富裕	well-to-do	E/I	49
gāojí	高级	senior	E/I	18
gèxìng	个性	personality	E/I	49
gōngdiàn	宫殿	palace	E/I	58
gōngláo	功劳	achievement	E/I	13
gòumǎi	购买	buy	E/I	42
guānyuán	官员	official	Adv	18
hángxíng	航行	sail	E/I	26
héfǎ	合法	legal	E/I	20
huàjiā	画家	painter	E/I	01
huánghòu	皇后	queen	Adv	11
hùnluàn	混乱	confusion	E/I	35
jìchéng	继承	inherit	E/I	35
jìmò	寂寞	loneliness	E/I	11
jìndài	近代	modern	E/I	48
jīngqí	惊奇	amaze	E/I	58
jìnǚ	妓女	prostitute	E/I	56

E/I = HSK Elementary / Intermediate Level
Adv = HSK Advanced Level

jìqiǎo	技巧	skills	E / I	*18*
láiyuán	来源	origin	E / I	*25*
liúchuán	流传	circulate	E / I	*60*
lóngzi	笼子	cage	E / I	*02*
mèngxiǎng	梦想	dream	E / I	*21*
míxìn	迷信	superstitious	E / I	*44*
nóngtián	农田	field	E / I	*25*
píngfán	平凡	homely, mediocre	E / I	*02*
pínkǔ	贫苦	poor	E / I	*28*
pǐnzhì	品质	quality	E / I	*27*
qǔ	娶	marry	E / I	*20*
quàngào	劝告	advise	E / I	*04*
quánlì	权力	power	E / I	*37*
rěnshòu	忍受	tolerate	E / I	*26*
shāngrén	商人	businessman	E / I	*49*
shēnfen	身份	identity	E / I	*12*
shēnyè	深夜	night	E / I	*26*
shìwù	事务	affairs	E / I	*42*
shōují	收集	collect	E / I	*18*
shuōfú	说服	persuade	E / I	*36*
tiāoxuǎn	挑选	choose	E / I	*02*
tíyì	提议	suggest	E / I	*60*
wēixiǎo	微小	little	E / I	*59*
xǐ'ài	喜爱	appeal to	E / I	*27*
xiézhù	协助	help	E / I	*19*
xìnrèn	信任	trust	E / I	*59*
xīnshì	新式	new	E / I	*29*
yǎngchéng	养成	cultivate	E / I	*10*

E / I = HSK Elementary / Intermediate Level
Adv = HSK Advanced Level

yìngfù	应付	handle	E / I	41
yuánlín	园林	garden	E / I	43
zàng	葬	bury	Adv	12
zhànlǐng	占领	occupation	E / I	58
zhēnguì	珍贵	precious	E / I	18
zhèngyì	正义	righteous	E / I	20
zǔzhǐ	阻止	prevent	E / I	36
gēxīng	歌星	singer	Adv	65
bàokān	报刊	newspaper	E / I	66
zázhì	杂志	magazine	E / I	66
hángyè	行业	industry	E / I	67
ǒurán	偶然	by chance	E / I	67
yùnqi	运气	luck	E / I	67
qīnrén	亲人	family member	E / I	12
zhuīqiú	追求	pursue	E / I	73
jǔbàn	举办	organize	E / I	74
hàoqí	好奇	curious	E / I	74
zìháo	自豪	proud	E / I	82
rènxìng	任性	headstrong	E / I	82
shènzhì	甚至	even	E / I	85
zhèngdǎng	政党	political party	E / I	85
chuàngzhào	创造	build	E / I	29
zhìhuì	智慧	wisdom	E / I	84
chābié	差别	difference	E / I	85
fēnliè	分裂	split up	E / I	85
dǎoyǎn	导演	director	E / I	91
xīnshǎng	欣赏	appreciate	E / I	19
pāishè	拍摄	make a movie	E / I	91

E / I = HSK Elementary / Intermediate Level
Adv = HSK Advanced Level

jiàzi	架子	arrogance	E / I	*92*
zhǎngshēng	掌声	applause	E / I	*66*
píngshěn wěiyuán	评审委员	selection committee member	Adv	*92*
zūnzhòng	尊重	respect	E / I	*74*
diǎnlǐ	典礼	ceremony	E / I	*93*
kǎoyàn	考验	challenges	E / I	*93*
tèwù	特务	secret agent	E / I	*94*
gāosù	高速	speedy	E / I	*94*

E / I = HSK Elementary / Intermediate Level
Adv = HSK Advanced Level